HIS FAVORITE GIRL

BRANDIE NIKOLE

DEDICATION

This book is dedicated to my love. Thank you for always encouraging me to work harder, inspiring me to be bolder and better, and for loving me through the pain as well as the joy. This book was made as a testimony to what you have shown me love can be.

CONTENTS

PROLOGUE

"Why are you not answering my calls?" I said as I pushed past Khalil into his apartment.

"Girl, you ain't call me. Stop lying." He chuckled as he closed the door and followed me into his kitchen. His roommate, Sean, was sitting at the counter, eating cereal.

I went to the refrigerator to get one of Khalil's smoothie drinks. "Wassup, Sean?" I spoke to his roommate.

"Wassup, Passion?" Sean replied as he laughed

I looked at Khalil with a frown. "Really, Khalil! Ugh."

"What?" he asked like he was innocent.

I just shook my head because we both knew only he could have told Sean my childhood nickname. I hated that nickname sometimes. It came from my mother. According to her, she called me Passion because I always give too much passion with everything I did, from dancing, to sassing her, to trying to sing.

Rolling my eyes at Khalil, I walked off and took the smoothie to his room. Khalil and I were sophomores at Florida A&M University, five hundred miles away from home, just the two of us. We've been close since grade school. It was always Ajah and Khalil. You never saw one without the other. However, we lived different lives here at college. I barely saw my friend, and I missed him. Khalil was a medical student, and I was majoring in hospitality and public relations. Preceding our freshman year, we started getting into our majors, and we couldn't schedule our classes together anymore. Plus, we both had full-time jobs, so there were no more playing. Things were happening, and we had to be on top of it all.

"Khalil, I'm feeling lonely. Can I stay here tonight?" I asked

"You know you can. There's no need to ask, but how you lonely when

I'm right here?" He chuckled, still standing by his room door.

"Don't laugh." I pouted. "I never see you. It's been like two weeks since we talked. You ain't missing me, bestie?"

"Girl, you trippin'. Stop being a brat. You know what we're doing here, but I feel ya tho. I miss seeing your big-head self too," he said with a titter.

There was a brief moment of silence between us, which never happens. I looked up from my entwined hands and stared right into Khalil's eyes. He was looking at me in a way I'd never seen before. It was strange.

"Come here," he said in his low baritone voice. For some unknown reason, I felt a quiver in my stomach.

I got up off his bed and went over to him, our eyes never wavering. When I made it to him, he encased me in his arms, and his big body covered mine. I squeezed him around his waist and buried my face in his chest.

"You know I'm always here, right?" Khalil mumbled into my hair

"I know. It's just sometimes I need to touch you. You're my only friend here. I don't have the time or desire to make any more. Just 'cause you are an athlete… med student and popular don't mean you get to forget about me," I whined into his chest

He laughed. "Whatever, girl. You know I'd drop anyone or anything for you."

When he said that, I raised my head to look up at him. It was something in his tone I didn't recognize. Once again, his eyes were transfixed on mine, and in them this time was lust and need. I looked at his lips, then back in his eyes. I begin panting. I knew he could feel my heartbeat. I could smell the mint on his breath we were so close.

He tilted his head down toward me. I lifted my eyes back to his. Next thing I knew, his lips were rubbing against mine, and then his tongue traced where his lips just were. I closed my eyes and inhaled. Then his lips covered mine. Full… sweet… juicy, those delicious lips were filled with so much passion. I gave him the same energy he was giving me. I would never tell him that he was my first tongue kiss. I would never share how much this moment changed my view of him as my friend. But most of all I will never forget what happened after he pulled back from our kiss, licked his lips, and looked me in my eyes then said "Damn, so you staying the night right?" all nonchalant.

In my mind, I already knew this was the night that would change our lives forever. Would it destroy our friendship or bring us closer was my biggest concern, because no matter what, I couldn't lose Khalil.

CHAPTER 1

Sitting in the living room of the five-bedroom, three-and-a-half-bathroom home I shared with my best friend in Texas, I immediately started laughing at him standing in the window with a frown on his face. I could hear him suck his teeth. As he began to speak, I looked up from my laptop at him. "Man… Ajah, this girl still went and got a blonde long weave in her head again after I told her I wanted to see her natural hair," he said with a scowl on his face.

"Boy, sit down. That's yo' boo," I replied with tears in my eyes from laughing so hard.

"You know how I am… man, I'll deal with that shit every now and then, but it's been eight months, and I still haven't seen her hair yet. She knows I like my babies natural with a lil' sassy," he said with a mischievous smirk on his face.

Shaking my head, I just bust out laughing.

Knock! Knock!

"Who is it?" Khalil's crazy self asked like he ain't been standing to the window in the foyer watching her get out of the car.

"Stop playing, Khalil. You know it's me. I just texted you," Khalil's girlfriend of the last eight months, Destiny, replied.

With a huff, he finally opened the door and stepped back to let her in.

"Hello, baby. How was your day?" Destiny said while giving him a kiss and while she side-eyed me at the same time. Behind her was Janyaa, her niece, and a puppy that I'd never seen before.

"What's up, miss Janyaa? Is this your dog?" asked Khalil.

"No, Auntie Destiny says this is you and her new baby," she replied with a huge smile on her face.

Janyaa was a beautiful little nine-year-old girl who followed her auntie in more ways than one, unfortunately. However, I doubted her dad—Destiny's big brother, Sean, who was one of the meanest men I ever met—knew what Auntie D was teaching little miss Janyaa. I'm sure if he did, their time together would be cut tremendously.

"Janyaa, your auntie is mistaken. I will never have a puppy, but you do not have to worry. I'll help her get everything straightened out," he stated.

I giggled while placing my face back into my laptop so I could finish booking my vacation for next week. I already knew my friend, and there was no way a puppy was going to be anywhere in his life plans. Khalil was not a pet person, same as me.

"Ugh, what you over there giggling about, Ajah? Always in somebody business," Destiny said with extra attitude.

"Watch yo' mouth and stop being disrespectful 'cause you're embarrassed. You know you should've talked to me before trying to bring that thing in my house," Khalil said angrily. "Janyaa, sweetie, go in the kitchen. Ajah baked some M&M cookies. Go get you a few while I speak with your auntie right quick."

"Yes, sir, Mr. K," replied Janyaa as she skipped into the kitchen—yet to acknowledge my presence but happy to eat my cookies. Good ole Auntie Destiny influence 101. I just shook my head.

As soon as her niece was out of the room, Destiny started pleading her case. "Baby, I didn't mean anything by what I said. Ajah knows we're cool. Hi! Girl, my bad. I'm just having a bad day. I apologize."

Although I peeped the fake lie she was throwing, I sweetly replied, "I have tough skin. You do not bother me at all. Apology accepted." With that, I closed my laptop, got up, and walked toward the stairs to the office Khalil and I shared.

Behind me, I heard them walking toward the kitchen, and Khalil asked, "When are you going to let me see your real hair? Did I not tell you I wanted to run my fingers through your hair when I see you? What you hiding under all this hair that you don't want me to see?"

"Boy. stop playing. You've seen my real hair before, and you can run your hands through this too, baby. Just no pulling," Destiny said with a chuckle

"Then what's the point, Destiny? I want the whole experience," he replied to her. That was the last I heard before closing the office door.

Khalil and I had been best friend since the sandbox after meeting up at school one day in the second grade. He was seven years old, and I was six years old. We became instant friends. Both of our mothers were on the PTA, so that only made us closer because we were at every school event together. Over the years, everyone, including our parents, had tried to make our relationship more than what it was like they couldn't grasp the idea that we are just the best of friends and nothing more.

Well, there was that one time in college our sophomore year at FAMU. We were both lonely and homesick. All we had was each other while we were away from our families, so we clung to that, letting it take us to a place I tried to forget almost daily. It's not that I regretted what we did, because I didn't. It was the fact that every time I tried to see past what we did, I could feel it on my skin, in my heart, and between my legs. It was only that one time though, and we both had moved past it. Our relationship had remained strong, and we weren't lonely anymore, so there was no need to live in the past. Khalil had Destiny, and I had Miami with my friend, Shavonne, next week. We were now two grown, successful individuals that happened to be best friend and roommates. Thank goodness we were able to get past what happened and still be in each other's life. I would be empty without my friend Khalil. Throughout our lives, we had experienced more than our fair share of extraordinary adventures, and I couldn't see me doing them with anyone else but him. Not even Shavonne could hold a candle to what I shared with Khalil.

And I just wanna hold you all night long
Whenever I'm around you, nothing's wrong
I'm hoping that you'll always be around
You got me on a high, I don't wanna come down
And I love it, I love it (these butterflies)
Yeah, I love it, I love it (I'm on a high)
Yeah, I love it, I love it
And I just wanna love on you (ooh)

Queen Naija knew she could sing. "Butterflies" was blasting through my headphones as I sat in the office, finishing up my paperwork for this bachelor party I was planning for a basketball player associate of Khalil's next month. Having my own event-planning business had been a dream come true. It didn't hurt that my best friend was a sports medicine doctor in a state that lived and breathed total sports, which allowed me to go to most of the parties and events he was invited to… perfect networking.

"Hey. You trying to go deaf?" Khalil said as he pulled my headphones away from my left ear.

"Oh, I was trying to focus on my work and block out any unwanted noise… my bad," I replied, my words dripping in sarcasm.

He chuckled. "What are you working on?"

"That bachelor party I'm planning in Houston next month. What you doing in here? Shouldn't you be knee-deep in something about now?" I said with a laugh.

"Naw, I'm just chilling. So, you ready for your trip next week? Do I need to take you to the airport, or what?" Khalil asked.

"Yes. I am booked and so ready for my fun-filled week in Miami. And no, you don't have to drop me off. I have the car service coming to get me," I said with a smirk already knowing what's coming.

"Man, you trippin'. I already took the day off. What time is your flight?"

5

he asked.

"It's at 1:15 in the afternoon," I replied.

"Alright. I'll be ready to drop you," he said, looking me directly in the eyes.

"Okay, big-head. If you must," I said with a slight smile.

That nervous feeling I had all those years ago came back full force. I cleared my throat.

"So what's up, Khalil? You got something on your mind. I can tell."

"I'm breaking up with Destiny," he said, totally knocking me over mentally.

"What!" I asked, shocked and excited at the same time.

"She's just getting to be with too much drama and bullshit antics. You know today with that puppy bullshit and everything, I'm just not feeling it anymore. It's like something is missing, and we're pushing to make this relationship something that it's not," he answered.

"I'm sorry to hear that. I thought you were happy with her," I said, trying to hide my smile.

"I thought so too, but lately, I just been feeling like I want to be single, especially with me traveling more with my job and everything," he said, once again looking me in the eyes.

"Yeah… I hear ya," I said, dropping my eyes from his.

"Don't sound all sad. You two can still be besties." He laughed while I just rolled my eyes.

"Shut up. You know that girl hates my guts, for whatever reason," I said.

With that, he just burst out laughing as he backpedaled out of the room. Shaking my head, I put my earbud back in my ear and let Pandora take me into the next few hours of organizing and planning. However, no matter how much Pandora I listened to, I couldn't shake the brief conversation Khalil and I just had out of my mind.

Trying not to overthink things, I threw myself into my work and focused on the beats and my paperwork 'cause I didn't want my mind drifting too far out of bounds. It might get dangerous.

CHAPTER 2

Though my flight from Texas was not very long, two hours and forty minutes to be exact, it was interesting to say the least. But I was finally here in the beautiful city of Miami!

I had stripped myself of all my clothes, taken a long, relaxing shower, and wrapped my hair in a towel to dry. As I lay sprawled out on the bed thinking, I let the blush-colored, goose-feather comforter on the king-sized bed I was in pull me into the oasis of its relaxation. Letting out a deep breath, I closed my eyes and tried my best to clear my mind and relax. I began to feel my mind being drawn to earlier today. I couldn't help it. I found myself thinking about my flight here. It wasn't the travel here in itself that had my mind in a frenzy; it was the event that occurred getting off the plane…

✱✱✱

"Oh! Excuse me," the little boy said to me after bumping me hard on my lower back and with such momentum that it pushed me forward, causing me to stumble.

I knew I was going to fall, especially in these four-inch stiletto heels, so I reflexively tried to grab the back of the seats to break the impact of my potential fall and the embarrassment it would cause. But before I could do so, I felt a set of smooth and soft muscle-clad arms grab a firm hold of me.

"I got you, beautiful," were the words I heard whispered into my right ear.

I looked at the arms that were holding me—solid, bulging biceps and vein-pulsating forearms with a beautiful display of colorful tattoos. I placed my hands on the arms wrapped around my waist and allowed my eyes to travel to its owner. As though I was in a trance, my eyes lingered on him for long seconds.

"Thank you," I said in a voice that did not sound like my own. I felt my heartbeat begin to elevate as I kept my eyes on him and quickly searched for my voice again. He helped me straighten myself upright, all the while, never removing his gaze from mine or his arms from around my body.

"Are you alright?" he asked in the sexiest, deep baritone voice.

Momentarily, a small shiver ran up and down my spine. "Yes. Thank you again for catching me," I said, looking back at him. He had these sexy, mocha-brown eyes that seemed to sparkle, and I found myself completely lost in them. It was as if they were looking right through me, speaking a symphony of the sweetest words to my soul. I heard myself gulp to try to catch my breath, and it wasn't from the near fall either. A silent breath escaped from between the crack of my lips. My heartbeat kept thumping through my chest. I was sure he could hear it too. The tingly shivers I was feeling caused intense chill bumps to materialize on my arms. I felt a sense of strange security in the arms of this man, whose name I didn't even know. He must have been reading my mind because as soon as I tried to move, his arms embraced me with a tight, welcomed squeeze. Involuntarily, a moan slipped from my lips. I instantly closed my eyes in embarrassment. Here I was, getting worked up by a complete stranger, letting him make me feel things I hadn't felt in as long as I care to remember.

As I opened my eyes, his grip loosened. The fantasy was over, and he was already making his stride halfway down the aisle from business class and off the plane. A part of me wanted to go after him, to get his name if nothing else, but the pride in me just made me stand there and stare. I stood in one place so long that the line in the aisle begin to move, and the area I was in became more crowded with people trying to get their luggage from the overhead compartment while others headed for the exit.

"Ugghh." I let out an exasperating breath in total frustration.

As I walked off the aircraft onto the jet bridge to get to the terminal, I stood on my tiptoes trying to catch a glimpse of Mister Strong Arms one more time, but his strides were long and powerful like his muscles that seemed to be protruding from under his shirt. And just that fast, he was out of sight. I guess he was in a hurry; that much was obvious.

"Damn," I said to myself.

It was disheartening, and I was furious at myself and the people in front of me for moving so damn slow, but mostly at him though. How dare he? Who did he think he was having me feel this way? And what the hell were these feelings anyway? I mulled these questions over in my head, all the while still thinking about him and the way he held me. I licked my lips and swayed my head left to right in disbelief. I really need to get laid. It's been way too long. Just as that thought crossed my mind, I heard my phone ping in my purse. Reaching inside, I pulled my phone out and saw I had an incoming text from Khalil.

Khalil: *Did you land yet?*

Me: *Just making my way to baggage claim, and then I gotta find Shavonne.*

Khalil: *A'ight bet... tell Sha I said hello, and don't have too much fun without me.*

Before I was able to respond to his last text my phone rang Beyoncé's "Run the World".

"Hello?" I quickly answered without checking, already knowing who it was from the ringtone.

"Hey, girl!" It was my best friend, Shavonne. "Where are you? You land yet?" she quickly asked. I was finally off the bridge path and in the terminal, speed walking to baggage claim. Shavonne was asking question after question, not giving me any chance to answer them. Her voice was filled with so much excitement that I couldn't do anything but smile as I listened to my friend go on and on.

It'd been a year since I'd been back home to visit. I was just too busy. She had finally managed to convince me to come to town. I was sure she was going to make it memorable as only Shavonne could. This trip was much needed for me, although I often traveled for my business. There was nothing like coming back to my hometown and catching up with friends and family. Furthermore, I needed some space from my roommate because I could feel myself slipping back into those dangerous fantasies that I tried to keep hidden.

I had to remind myself to visit my parents, as well as Khalil's, while I was here. My mother and father actually came to visit me in Texas a couple months ago before they went to Paris, and I was anxious to see what they brought me back.

Shavonne kept on talking and talking, telling me how much fun we were going to have. Her enthusiasm for our time together was contagious. She was such a good friend to me, no matter how many states were between us. Listening to all the plans she had for us during my stay reminded me how much she was still the adventurous woman I'd always known her to be. I knew I was definitely taking some stories back home with me to share. Khalil was going to be jealous.

I tried to cut her off to let her know where I was, but before I could muster up the words, I noticed Mister Strong Arms about to get in a car outside. He momentarily turned his head, and our eyes locked on each other's.

He smiled.

I blushed with delight.

The pounding of my heart escalated.

He teasingly licked his luscious ass, plump lips, then got in a red Challenger sitting at the curb.

Faintly, I could hear my friend calling my name on the phone. "Ajah...

Ajah!" she yelled. But I could not respond. I was stuck in a trance of both awe and bewilderment. Nothing seemed to be making any sense right now. As he was about to drive away, he let the window down, looking out of the car one more time. He fixed his mesmerizing, brown eyes on me, as though to let me know he saw me staring at him. I couldn't blink if I wanted to. He had me, and then he sent a wink my way. I quickly turned my head in an attempt to be nonchalant about the ordeal. And just as I tilted my chin up to get one last look, he was gone.

"Damn." I cursed to myself a little too loud, forgetting I was on the phone still.

"Wha-What's wrong?" asked Shavonne in my ear.

"Nothing, girl," I replied swiftly to avoid the barrage of questions that I knew were to follow. "Where are you at? I'm at baggage claim number twenty-six," I asked, remembering the last thing she said to me.

I looked around to see if I could see her. She was describing where she was, but her short five-five self was lost in the sea of people moving about the airport. I stood still and strained on my toes to get extra leverage of height to find her. Then it happened. I heard her before I could get a complete full view of her…

"Passionnnnn!" she yelled my nickname into the phone and in the crowd.

There she stood, waving her hands in the air, my beautiful friend… my sister. Gorgeously displaying her mocha-colored skin, bowed legs, wide hips, slim waist, and a long, red, curly afro that reached the middle of her shoulder blades, she was dressed in a lime-green-and-white striped short romper looking like a whole meal. My face lit up with anticipation. We began to make our way toward one another, navigating through the crowd of people in exaggerated haste. I was having a hard time maneuvering with my luggage, and jogging in the heels I was wearing was not making it any easier. I could hear her approach getting closer. The fact that she was shouting "excuse me" loudly along the way also helped.

However, it was what followed after the last excuse me that caused all movement and sounds closest to me to come to a screeching halt.

"Boy, don't you play with me!" a voice that sounded a lot like Shavonne's shouted extremely loud. I, along with many other patrons, stared in the direction of her voice. Then there was a slap.

Slap!

When I got about a foot closer, I noticed that it was indeed Shavonne, facing some guy. She was berating him embarrassingly, jabbing her finger at him and shoving him backward by pushing both of her hands into his chest. The guy had her in both weight and height, but he seemed too shamed and shocked to do anything other than stare at her.

"I am a grown ass woman, and just because it's big, you do not have the right to grab it! I am not yours!" Shavonne yelled while pointing at the guy.

He just stood there for a couple minutes, fuming with rage. "You got that, ma. My bad."

"You right, yo' bad"

"Let me make it up to you. Give me your number. Let me take you out sometime?" he asked, licking his lips, looking Shavonne up and down.

Was this dude for real? Didn't she just slap him in the middle of the airport, and he was still was trying to holla?

"No. thank you… I'll pass," Shavonne said, turning her back, dismissing him.

Her ass was so rude.

"You got that, ma. Yo' loss." And with that he shrugged and walked off.

The stunned crowd dispersed as well, snickering and whispering under their breath as they passed.

"Shavonne, girl, what happened?" I asked, humor laced in my tone.

"Girl, nothing," she replied with a slight angered tone in her voice.

Grabbing my arm, she guided us out of the airport. I pulled myself from her grasp and gave her that "you better answer me" look.

"That fool had the nerve to grab my ass as I was walking by. Then his disrespectful behind gonna ask me how much, like I'm some prostitute or thot."

"Girl, you should have let me know all that before bringing me out here. We about to jump his ass!" I said furiously, trying to head back into the airport.

She just started hugging me real tight around my waist preventing me from going back and laughed. "He ain't worth it, sis." With that, I calmed down and began laughing too.

I threw my arm around her shoulder, and we walked toward the parking area to get in her brand-new 2019 Jeep Wrangler.

CHAPTER 3

I woke up with a plethora of energy. The nap I took did my body good and gave me the energy I needed for whatever adventures awaited me. I spread my arms out wide, took a deep breath, and stretched prevailingly, taking in the delightful aura of this beautiful city. Shavonne's condo was directly across from the beach. I could see the sun setting right over the balcony in the guestroom I was in. The sunny warmth of South Beach's weather drifted throughout the room in a majestic grandeur, carrying with it a sense of peace and tranquility.

It was refreshing. I jumped out of the bed, full of newly-found calmness and began looking for something comfortable to wear.

Shavonne walked into the house. "Passion, you up?" she called out. She was so loud that if I was still sleeping, she would've woken me up.

"Well, if I wasn't, I am now," I replied back to her jokingly.

"Whatever. What are you doing?" Shavonne asked, giving me a questionable look as she stepped into the room.

"I'm looking for something to wear. I'll be out in a second," I said as I walked into the closet where I placed my clothes earlier. After that, my plan was to head into the bathroom to do my hygiene and wash my face.

She didn't wait for me to come out. Instead, she just burst into the walk-in closet, opening the door wider. Hearing the door hit the wall, I turned my head in her direction and laughed at her. She stood in the doorway, looking at me with a wide smile.

"What your crazy self up to?" I asked her while still laughing.

"I wanna go out tonight. There's this new club opening up on the strip called Club Iconic. You had your nap, and now I wanna party with my friend," she said with her lips poked out.

"I'm down. Just let me find something else to wear." I agreed with her request, going further into the closet toward the back.

"Yay! Okay. I'm going to get ready too," she said over her shoulder as she skipped out the room.

I just laughed to myself. That girl was a handful. Good thing I loved her like I did. Soon as I walked out the closet heading into the bathroom, my phone starting vibrating and ringing on the bed. Looking at the screen, I saw Khalil's name.

"Hello there, sir. Miss me already?" I said as I answered, finally walking into the bathroom with the phone.

"Nope. But you never texted me back," he replied.

"That was hours ago… really, Khalil? It took you a long time to care about my well-being." I sassed, not liking his response.

"I figured you and Shavonne were catching up, so I was giving you time, but my patience ran out," said Khalil.

"Awww, you do miss me," I replied, now smiling.

His reply was just him chuckling. "What you ladies up to?" Khalil asked, changing the subject, not responding to me.

"Getting dressed to go out," I said, dancing by myself in the mirror.

"Don't let me hold you up then. I'm good now that I know you're safe," Khalil said. "Be good tonight and send me a picture. Let me see you dressed up."

What! I thought to myself.

I pulled the phone from my ear to make sure I was talking to Khalil. That has never been a request from him before, and it threw me off guard. Trying to play it nonchalant, I replied, "Okay, I got you!"

"Bet, talk to you tomorrow." I could hear the smile in his voice in his reply.

"Alright. Good night." With that, I hung up.

I couldn't help the smile that remained on my face after talking to Khalil. I really needed to get me some other male attention. I was finding myself having thoughts that were long ago put away, and it could really complicate life as I knew it now.

***

Ready to hit the town, I walked out of the bedroom feeling like a supermodel.

"Well, hello, Miss Hot Thing!" Shavonne said admiringly as I walked out of the room "You trying to catch something tonight?" She finished as she gave a final fix to my clothes.

I smiled, looked her over, and said, "You're the one to talk. You look like you had some but trying to get some more." I laughed.

I had on a white knit dress that came down just above my knee with a slit on both thighs complemented with a long-sleeved, red leather jacket and my

Christian Louboutin So Full Kate studded, leather booties. The dress hugged my body nicely. It accentuated my curves and long legs. I wasn't showing too little, yet again, I wasn't showing too much either. I was the sexy, casual one that was not to be forgotten nor was I trying to get in too much trouble… I hoped.

Shavonne was wearing a short, peach skirt that stopped mid-thigh with a black, lace blouse that exposed most of her back. On her feet were Christian Louboutin Metrolisse over-the-knee leopard boots with a leopard clutch to match. Her makeup was immaculately flawless. My friend was glowing like she had gotten some and was trying to get some more for real.

Facing one another, we looked each other over approvingly, then gave ourselves some final touches on the mirror hanging in her living room. After snapping a few pictures for Khalil and social media, we grabbed our essentials and walked out the door.

"You ready to turn up, sis?" she asked as we walked out the door.

"Hell yeah!" I answered, high-fiving her.

CHAPTER 4

Coming to the block of the club, velvet ropes lined the street, then vanished, only to return under new blinking signs that read *Club Iconic*. Occupying those ropes was a long line of clubbers, vying to be let in.

"Damn, girl. How are we supposed to get in?" I exclaimed to her upon seeing the long line.

She threw her arms around me, then gave me a mischievous yet playful smile and said, "Don't worry. I got us."

She urged me forward, and we walked past the line and people that started to mumble and strain to see if we were going to get turned back around to join them in the line. Walking side by side with her, I hoped against the odds that could disable us that we would not get embarrassed. *I'd kill her*, I thought to myself.

"C'mon, sis," she urged on.

My feet felt as though they were covered by concrete, and I was being dragged against my will. But I pressed forward, not that I had a choice with Shavonne pulling me to the front door. To my surprise, she walked up to the bouncer, leaned forward and kissed him on the cheek.

"Hey, Tim," I heard her say. "This is my sister, Passion." She introduced me.

He looked over at me with curiosity as well as a look of interest and winked. I threw him a head nod. I could tell he was undressing me with his eyes.

I turned my head, smiling faintly to seem unaffected by his up-and-down assessment and stare. "Why the hell am I blushing? I'm falling off," I mumbled to myself as I turned my head back around to face Shavonne and Tim.

"I didn't know you had a sister," he said to her while looking at me lustfully, licking his lips and rubbing his big, meaty hand through his beard.

"A fine one too!" He winked again.

"Hey! Now you know better." Shavonne chastised him while snapping her fingers at him "So don't play." She rolled her neck

"Alright... alright. No need to get all hood chick on me, baby" he said, laughing. He let us through the velvet rope while saying, "Y'all have fun, okay!"

"Always, Tim... Always, baby." Shavonne fired back while blowing him a kiss.

I looked back at the line and saw some of the women still standing in line fuming with animosity at how we just skipped them and was let in. *Ha, line huggers!* I mused to myself, relieved that we didn't have to be in that long line or waiting for some hotshot to get us in with them.

The doors opened, and instantly, the ambiance of the club hit me. It was like walking into a mansion with the grandest state-of-the-art features, like beautiful chandeliers. The atmosphere was unlike any I'd experienced in a club. It felt inviting with a keen sense of elegance and class. The colors gold, black, and white made up the décor. A dense vapor of smoke drifted throughout as flashing lights swayed to the rhythm of the hypnotic beat the DJ was playing while illuminating the dance floor. Acrobatic women were suspended in the air, performing their rituals. Spiral stairs came in and out of sight, leading to floating VIP booths. The waitresses, dressed in black leather tights with matching corset outfits, were meticulously navigating through the crowd with lit bottles and trays of drinks to serve. It was a final destination of party utopia.

As the music shifted and flames erupted on the stage dramatically, Cardi B's "Money" began to play in the background. The crowd roared, shouting out their approval of the music. Those that weren't there already gave up holding the wall and made their way to the colossal dance floor, gyrating energetically against each other. Feeling the hype of the music, Shavonne and I danced our way into the crowd, unable to resist the energy coming that surrounded us.

We dance carelessly, swaying our hips from side to side. Not long after hitting the floor, two men came to dance with us. The one dancing with Shavonne was light skinned with a lot of piercings. It went with his look though. He was handsome. My dancing partner had tattoos all over his visible skin, including his pecan-tan face. He was cute but not my type. Nevertheless, we allowed them to enjoy our moves as we winded and twerked to the beat provocatively.

I looked over at Shavonne and smiled as she nods her head and sings to the words. "All a bad bitch need is the money!"

I could feel the guy I was dancing with begin getting a hard-on. It made me look over my shoulder at him and take a step forward. *He tried it*, I thought to myself.

"Everybody enjoying themselves!" yelled the DJ, keeping everybody hyped up.

"Yeahhhhh!" was the response from the crowd, throwing their hands in the air.

"Hey, let's get something to drink," I said to Shavonne, feeling a little parched.

"OK!" she responded.

We left the dance floor and headed to the bar. The bartender served us our drinks. We both ordered Wallbangers. The two guys we were dancing with came over, then surprised us both by paying for our drinks. After we thanked them, we chatted with them for a few minutes before they walked off pissed because we did not give them our numbers when they asked. Their names were Benz and Supreme. And although they seemed nice enough, piercings and tattoos on the face were definitely not our cup of tea.

"They don't give up down here," I said to Shavonne after turning another guy that was standing close to us at the bar down.

Not to sound boastful, but I knew I was fine standing five-eight with cherry-Cola-colored, natural, curly long hair down my back, a caramel blessed skin tone, hazel eyes with a speck of gray, slim waist, enough ass to cuff, and some baby-making hips with thick thighs. I could definitely pull me any man I wanted. I haven't earned my six-pack yet, but I was a regular in the gym five days a week, and I ran at least six miles a day. So I was used to men approaching me, and I mean that in the humblest way possible. But I also had to be attracted to him, and none of the men I'd seen tonight met my standard in the looks department, especially after meeting Mister Strong Arms. They had to come with it when stepping to me.

She laughed at me, then said, "Girl, you haven't seen nothing yet. They just getting started," she had the nerve to say, like she wasn't already hugged up with a guy I chuckled at her and shook my head Turning my back to them, I surveyed the crowd on the dance floor and then turned around to face the entrance door.

Suddenly, the front door opened, and my eyes lingered on it for longer than I cared to admit. A rush of outside light crept inside and splash across my face. But my eyes didn't falter. They stay fixated there, almost as if I was expecting or waiting for someone specific to come through it. The silhouette of a body appeared before my eyes, and just as it appeared, it vanished.

"Damn," I whispered. I didn't get a chance to make out the face before the door closed, and the light from outside was gone.

After standing in a daze for a couple minutes, just daydreaming, I hear, "How you doing, queen?" from behind me. The voice sounded somewhat familiar with a sexy accent. I thought it must have been someone I danced with before and turned them down.

"Listen," I started to say, "I'm not—" I wasn't able to complete what I was going to say. All of a sudden, turning him down became a laborious task I did not want to perform. Words suddenly had abandoned my lips, taking with them my voice along with the composure of my beating heart, leaving in its place a sudden flutter of tingly feelings. I couldn't believe my eyes. But I was glad at what they were seeing.

Standing there, looking as sexy as ever, was none other than Mister Strong Arms from the airplane. Standing at what has to be about six-four, he had on a pair of black slacks with a white-pinstripe, long-sleeved dress shirt with the first two top buttons undone, exposing the Cuban link chain that seemed to be anchored by his large muscular chest. Complementing his attire was a blazer that seemed to showcase his masculinity. To say that I was happy to see him again would be an understatement. Time seemed to have slowed down as I stood here like a fool staring at him.

The crowd surged around us in a blur, as my field of vision narrowed. All I saw was him. My mouth was agape in disbelief, and I became shy. Words fled from me, but I continued to look at him fondly. I bit the corner of the inside of my lips and smiled. Feeling the plexus of my brain rejoicing, I got off the stool to stand, but I had wobbly legs like I've been riding the bull for fifteen minutes. Standing with a confident stance, I closed the short distance between us, and now we were both smiling and gazing into each other's eyes.

"Hi," he said. His eyes, the color of seduction, were like a magnetic force that felt like it was constantly tugging at me, pulling me closer to him.

"H-Hi," I stammered, struggling to retain a piece of myself.

We continued to gaze at each other as if no one else existed around us. We weren't conscious of it, but now it seems obvious. We were far along in a mating dance whose steps we all follow but few of us understand. Certainly, he and I didn't understand it, but we were dancing as hard as we could yet still apart.

"I'm Malachi," he said, extending his hand for me to shake.

Still feeling overwhelmed with gladness, I happily placed my hand in his and say, "I'm Passion." I wasn't giving up the real name just yet.

With his mesmerizing eyes remaining on mine, he lifted my hand up to his mouth and kissed the back of it. The gesture was both flattering and electrifying. Interestingly enough, though, sparks of electricity darted through sacred parts of my being, causing friction between my thighs. My face turned scarlet as my eyes finally broke free from the allure of his captivity, inadvertently closing. My lips helplessly parted, allowing the tip of my tongue to trace the coating of its outline.

Damn. What the hell was he doing to me? I thought weakly as thoughts and images bedazzled my consciousness.

"It's a pleasure to meet you, queen," he said, letting go of my hand.

I felt torn. Struggling with my mind and my body, I cleared my throat and reluctantly took back my hand. My eyes landed on his lips, and I instantly wondered the feel of them on my body.

"Wow," he said, catching my marveling eyes again. "You are absolutely gorgeous, like a blossomed lotus in the autumn," he recited while rubbing his left hand along my jawline.

I blushed right away. It was cute—corny but cute—and with his voice carrying on like thunder to a quiet storm, strong and powerful yet very gentle, it left me speechless. "Thank you," I said, unable to hide my happiness. "You don't look too bad yourself."

"Oh, is that right?" he said with smiling eyes of amusement,

With my clutch bearing the brunt of my excitement through my hands, I crossed my wrists in front of me, slightly rose an eyebrow, straightened my posture, and watched as he gracefully took another crafted step closer to me. He was so close now I could smell his cologne. Or perhaps I'd been smelling him all along and didn't know it. He smelled good. I felt myself gravitating toward him as he continued to enrapture me to weakness with his tantalizing smile.

"Maybe," I responded teasingly.

He laughed, amused by the little cat games I was playing with him.

"Well…" he said, shortening his light, infectious laugh. "I wanted to apologize for leaving so abruptly back at the airport—"

I quickly cut him off, placing my hand on his bulging arms at the same time and saying, "I'm the one who should be apologizing. I didn't get to thank you for saving me from the embarrassment of falling flat on my face."

"How'd you like to make it up to me over dinner tomorrow?" Malachi said in a smooth, chivalrous yet stern voice. "Say eight o'clock?"

Before I could answer, two men approached him from behind. One stopped short as the other, equally as tall and immaculately well-dress as Malachi, faced him, partially blocking my sight to him and whispered something only he could hear in his ear. I watched as he made a motion with his head, and the guy left him.

"I apologize for that," he said, motioning to the guy that had impolitely interrupted our conversation.

"Something has come up that I personally need to go take care of," he stated.

"It's cool," I replied, attempting to show that I was unfazed.

"So how about it, gorgeous? Would you like to have dinner with me tomorrow night?"

"I would like that very much, handsome," I answered

He smiled. We exchanged numbers and made promises to see each other tomorrow. Gradually, with a burden of hesitation, he began to walk away. A part of me wanted to stop him, grab his arm, throw myself onto him, and go with him, even just so I could be in his presence. But I did nothing, just watched as the crowd, which seemed to suddenly reappear out of nowhere, began to swallow him.

He paused briefly and looked back at me, staring for long minutes. I almost thought he'd come back toward me, but he didn't, just winked, turned, and walked completely up into the VIP section.

Staggered by foreign emotions, I turned my head to collect myself but quickly returned them to where I last saw him. I was left overwhelmed with carnal passion, pining for yet unseen, even as I watched Malachi disappear into the surging traffic of the VIP section.

CHAPTER 5

It was hard watching him leave, yet I stood there, unable to move my legs and go after him like every part of my being was screaming, provoking even, for me to do. Unable to open my mouth and call out to him or to even divert my pitiful gaze, the crowd began to swarm around at such a rapid pace that I thought was unfair. Surely, they must have a vendetta against me, I thought. I was mad at myself. I secretly cursed the crowd for being so cruel, and him—although he'd never know it—for being so enigmatically attractive. His sensual nearness, however brief, was already missed for as he'd completely disappear from my longing sight, images of him began to infiltrate my mind. I inwardly wished tomorrow would hurry up and get here.

I didn't know what else to do. One thing was for sure, I didn't want to be here anymore. But I didn't want to leave just yet either. So I stayed where I was for a moment more, wishing and hoping that he would materialize from the cruel engorging crowd and walk up to me, wrap me in his arms, and tell me he changed his mind.

But he never came back.

Feeling apathy, I scanned the crowd looking for Shavonne. She was cuddled up with some redbone, tall guy, and that was the moment I knew I was ready to go. I didn't want to mingle with anyone else, and I didn't want to be a third wheel.

"Hey, girl, you ready to leave?" I asked while walking over to Shavonne, not leaving any room that stated otherwise.

"No." She said sucking her teeth.

"Well, I am. However, if you're not, that's cool. I'll just take an Uber back to the spot," I said, not fazed by her response.

"Naw, party pooper we don't do split ups. We came together; we leave together… Let's go," she said.

Turning back to the guy she was all hugged up with, she said "I'll holla at you later, Zo."

"Let me walk y'all out. If you bouncing, I'ma head out too," Zo replied.

With that, we all walked toward the door. Zo was stopped midway to the door by someone he knew after us declining to wait on him, Shavonne and I parted ways with him. Shavonne gave him a kiss on the cheek, and he squeezed her tight and whispered something in her ear that had her cheesing hard. I was definitely asking her about Mr. Zo when we get back to her condo. After saying goodbye to her new friend and promising to hit his number later, we left. Although I was hoping to be stopped by Malachi on the way out, I had no such luck.

The bouncer at the door, Tim, tried to engage in conversation with us when we came out, asking why we were leaving so early. But Shavonne covered for me and said, "Boy, it's two in the morning. It's not early. It's late. Plus, I have meetings to attend in the morning."

Not wanting to fight, he conceded and gave us both a hug and said, "Y'all be safe."

Standing on the sidewalk of the club, walking toward Shavonne's car, out of my peripheral, I noticed a black Bentley parked right behind the valet stand.

"Damn, girl! That's a sexy ride!" Shavonne said with full neck-roll animation.

As soon as she said that, my phone vibrated in my clutch. I pulled it out, thinking it may have been Khalil checking on us again. Instead, it was a message from an unknown number.

954-484-1094: *Can't wait to see you tomorrow are you as anxious as I am!*
Me: *Who is this?*
954-484-1094: *Your future…*
Me: **thinking emoji* I doubt that.*
954-484-1094: *LOL! Look to your left, baby.*

I stopped, turned my head, then curiously looked at the Bentley that was to my left at the curb. Shavonne walked a few steps ahead of me but stopped when she saw that I had stop walking.

"What's wrong?" she asked, looking at the car too.

I said nothing just turned to face the car while looking back at my phone to see if another unknown message came through. Nothing. I began to look left, then right to see where he was or was he actually in the Bentley like I assumed.

Abruptly, the car door opened, and a tall figure stepped out. With the cell phone light illuminating in the dark, there exposed no other than Mister Strong Arms himself, Malachi. Similar to a high-school girl with the biggest crush on the most popular star player in school, I felt flustered with excitement. My heartbeat quickened as he began to walk toward me. Impulsively, I began to walk toward him also.

As we were slowly getting closer to each other, a group of people came bursting out the door two guys came rushing behind me. One of them shoved me to the ground and laughed, saying, "Move the fuck on, thirsty ass hoe."

Before I had the chance to do or say anything, Malachi ran up to him, grabbed him by the collar of his shirt, lifted him clean off his feet, and slammed him on his back to the ground. He pulled a gun from his waist and pressed it against the guy's forehead. He hit him over the head with the butt of the gun.

"Motherfucker, how the fuck you suppose I'm going to continue to allow you to live after you just disrespected my woman? You must not know my name. I'll kill you."

I was overwhelmed with a mix of emotions. I was pissed and angry and at the same time hurt and embarrassed. But with all that, I was a slightly aroused hearing Malachi protecting my honor and calling me his woman—a memo I did not get by the way, being that I just learned his name. Who did he think he was? He didn't even know me to be calling me his woman. Yet hearing it made me feel a sense of giddiness. Yeah, I'm tripping.

It was obvious that the guy was scared. The fact that he now smelled of shit also proved that to be evident. His friends who were with him had left running when they'd seen the gun. There was a big gash on his head from where Malachi hit him with the pistol, causing blood to leak from his head down the side of his face.

A small crowd had gathered a little distance down the sidewalk trying to see what was going on. I'd gotten up with the aid of Shavonne but stood off to the side trying to see what Malachi was going to do to the guy. He got up off the guy and kicked him in his stomach and said, "Now apologize to my girl, and it better be sincere."

"I'm so sorry, ma'am," the guy said with pleading eyes. I didn't reply, just rolled my eyes.

"Get the fuck out of here, pussy, before I end you," Malachi stated after kicking him again.

With one hand holding his stomach and the other the back of his head, the guy stumbled away.

As if nothing had happened, Malachi walked over to me, and with his still-captivating, seductive tone, he said, "Are you alright, gorgeous?"

I nodded my head up and down. "So I'm your woman now, huh?" I asked with a chuckle.

He chuckled and cupped the sides of my face in his hands, caressing it with feather-light touches and then pinched my chin with his fingers to adjust it to look into his big, mocha-brown gaze.

"Forget me already?" he asked with a calm allure.

Before I could even answer, Shavonne ditzy ass said, "Forgetting you would be impossible. However, we haven't met yet. I would love to get to know you… uh—"

I laughed so hard my head fell behind me.

Smiling, Malachi pulled my face back to him and said, "No, beautiful. I was speaking to the marvelous woman standing in front of me."

She looked at me with the side-eye. "Wow, Passion. You've done well, my little grasshopper." She joked.

We all laughed. My friend, I couldn't take her anywhere.

"No. I didn't forget you at all. I just didn't know that when we exchanged numbers and names it had amplified your position in my life," I said while smiling all big.

"Amazing how positions can be elevated in just a blink of an eye," he replied with a smirk.

"Well, we were just leaving, and to answer your question… yes, I'm looking forward to it as well." I winked.

Taking a step backward out of his grasp, I grab Shavonne's hand, then turn around giving him my back and walked away, leaving him to admire me from the back as I strolled teasingly away from him. I heard him chuckling behind us. I made sure to put a little more sway in my strut, giving him something to think about until tomorrow. *Let that hold ya*, I thought, amusing myself.

To say the ride back to Shavonne's was a quiet one would be a lie. I filled her in on all things Malachi, and she smiled the entire time, saying we're going shopping because she has to make sure my attire matches the Bentley-appreciable attraction. That made me laugh uncontrollably, but I told her I concurred.

I spent the rest of the night thinking and daydreaming about what was to come tomorrow on my date with Malachi. It felt like the coming of the first day of school. I was filled with excitement. Not because of the Bentley he was driving or status, but because he'd come to my defense and called me his woman, something I knew nothing about. Or did I? There was this irresistible attraction to him that I felt drawn to. I couldn't wait to see what he had planned for our night.

✳✳✳

It felt surreal riding down the streets of Miami. The flow of the palm trees in the wind and the smell of the ocean right outside the window reminded me of the things I missed about living here. With all the Destiny and Khalil drama that was going on back home in Texas, I needed this getaway. After speaking with Khalil this morning while I laid in bed, before Shavonne came to get me to go shopping for tonight, he informed me that he finally broke it off with Destiny, and now she was popping up at the house and knocking on the door all hours of the night to the point that he had to have the guards at our entrance to void her once open pass.

I was happy to be away from all of that because I could only imagine now that he ended their union how the real Destiny was going to be coming out. I can't say I blamed her. Khalil was the ultimate catch—a successful, *black* millionaire, close to billionaire by now; six-five ; 245lbs of pure muscle; smooth, milk-chocolate skin with tattoos that graced his chest and arms so beautifully it was like he was born with them; honey-brown eyes, and full, sexy ass lips. He was full of class and smarter than anybody I knew with some of that hood swag we all loved and charm that would make you want to drop your panties immediately after having a conversation with him. He was always an impeccable dresser. From suits to jeans, he could rock anything. If he wasn't my best friend, I'd be definitely trying to shoot my shot. *Stop thinking like that!* I chastised myself.

"What you over there thinking so hard about?" Shavonne asked, breaking me from my thoughts.

"Just some mess Khalil told me about earlier regarding him and his boo, Destiny," I said with a laugh. Shavonne couldn't stand Destiny either. She knew she was no good for Khalil.

"Ugh! I can't stand that rat," Shavonne said about Destiny with her face in a frown.

"Well, we don't have to worry about her coming on trips no more. He gave her walking papers," I replied.

"Good! Now you and Khalil can stop playing house and finally get together," she stated while giving me the side-eye trying to see how I would respond.

"How are you gon' just put us together?" I asked her.

"'Cause I know the both of you," she said, leaving that powerful statement in the wind for me to contemplate on.

"So where to first? I'm ready to shop and then go take a nap," I said, changing the subject.

"Mmmhmm." Shavonne knew what I was doing. "I ain't with all that shopping. Let's hit Neiman's first tho. They had these YSL platform pumps I saw online I gots to have," she said with enthusiasm.

"Now you speaking my language," I replied with a smile.

After riding in silence for about five minutes, which I knew was killing her 'cause she loved having the last word, Shavonne said, "Let me say this though, Ajah, you have to do what makes you happy and not try to stay inside of this imaginary glass box. You and Khalil have a friendship, but you also have a history. You told that man you wanted to move to Texas, and he made sure you had everything you needed and that you stayed in his home although you could've… shit he would've bought you one of your own," Shavonne said.

"That's what friends do for each other, Shavonne. What you saying?" I sassed.

"I'm saying, everybody knows y'all in love but y'all, and you need to start living for your happiness and go after what you want," she replied with a slight neck roll.

"Whatever, Sha! Don't be fucking with my head before my date. We can do serious talk another day, okay?"

"Yeah, I got you," she replied, and with that, she turned her music up as we continued our journey to Aventura Mall while Lil' Durk's "India" played on blast... Go figure.

CHAPTER 6

Anticipation made it an extremely long countdown to this moment, but at last, it had arrived! I'd spent the time waiting, cleaning, and rearranging some of Shavonne's things around her home for no reason but to just kill the time. Music had been playing along as we sipped on Stella Rose champagne and danced. Shavonne was making all sorts of silly remarks about the date to come, making nasty jokes regarding sex, and saying I was finally going to kill the sexual drought I've been in. I assured her that was not going to happen, and she laughed at me wholeheartedly, not believing the lie I was trying to sell her as well as myself.

I had gotten a text from Malachi earlier telling me to wear something comfortable. When I asked him like what, he just said something comfortable… men. Doesn't he know that I need more information to prepare? Ugh.

So I decided to call him to get a solid idea, more so to hear the sound of his voice too, though. He'd picked up with a laugh, and I was instantly filled with the excitement of anticipation. He had me all coy, and I didn't know how he was doing so.

"Hello?" he answered, still with the laugh in his voice.

"You know I need more details beside dress comfortable. Our ideas of comfortable can be totally different," I replied, smiling.

"Baby, you could wear a sweat suit and be sexy to me… don't stress about dress code, ya feel me?" he said.

"Baby, huh? You moving mighty fast, but I'll give you that. I won't stress. I'll just go with the flow." I chuckled.

"You ready for me, though? I'll be there soon. Just finishing up some things, and I'ma come scoop you." He smoothly changed the subject.

"I'll be ready by our agreed-upon time… yes, Malachi." I sassed.

"Yeah… I love how you say my name," he said with a chuckle.

"I bet you do." I laughed. "Don't start what you may not be able to finish."

"If I ain't nothing else, I'm all man. A challenge has never scared me, lil' baby."

"We shall see, Mr. Malachi! See you in a few." I teased.

"Straight up… One." Just like that, he hung up.

Shavonne was letting me have it with her jokes saying that I was caking and cheesing like a schoolgirl.

As the hours dwindled down to minutes, I suddenly found myself rushing to get ready. Excited, I quickly brushed my teeth and jumped in a hot shower. It was so hot that when I came out, steam was leaving my body. Then I started moisturizing my body with some sweet-smelling coconut oil lotion Shavonne made me buy when we went shopping. I tried on outfit after outfit until I finally settled on a lace, burgundy bodycon dress that highlighted my curves nicely. I bought it earlier at the mall. I paired it with a black, leather-pocket, fitted jacket. Shavonne came in shouting compliments on how good I looked, then picked out a sexy set of open-toed Michael Kors Blaze booties that she thought would complete the outfit.

At 7:55 p.m., with five minutes to spare, there was a knock at the door. Prompt, I liked that. What Shavonne and I were doing to get me ready came to an immediate halt. We looked at each other momentarily. I felt flustered. Through my body was the rush of anticipation and excitement. The knock came again.

Knock! Knock! Knock!

I hurried to finish getting ready.

"I'll get it," Shavonne said, leaving me in the room.

After a couple minutes and a few deep breaths, I came out of the room. What greeted me left me speechless. The sight of Malachi's eyes observantly looking upon me was breathtaking. He had this huge smile on his face. I stopped short to admire his brazen shoulders bulging from under the royal-blue-and-white-striped Ralph Lauren shirt that seemed to be clinging to him in all the right places, with a pair of dark-blue Levi jeans. He looked sexy and comfortable. I was pleased with the showmanship. I smirked at the sexual thoughts that crossed my mind in that instant.

"Hello, beautiful. You look amazing," he said, smiling.

My face suddenly was rushed with a wave of heat. If I was a few shades lighter, he'd see my blush. "Why, thank you!" I said, smiling as I walked over and hugged him.

He smelled good. He was wearing Jean Paul Gaultier Le Male. I'd know that smell anywhere. I inhaled, trying to sneak a sniff from his body. At that moment, I began to feel my nipples get hard. He gently rubbed his face against mine, and my skin began to tingle from his hair brushing my skin… He took a sniff of my hair, and I felt a tremor deep within.

"You are absolutely gorgeous," he whispered in my ear.

The tremoring sound in his deep voice in my ear made it obvious that he was struggling, as I was, to restrain himself from giving in to his desires. He kissed my ear, then moved down to my cheek. His lips lightly grazed mine. I opened mine faintly to welcome his. But it never came. *Dammit.* We were both oblivious to everything around us. He stared into my eyes and pecked my lips, then began to whisper his sweet nothings against them. He was making love to my mind, and I did not know how to respond. I felt like the world was blending into a rhythm of his absolute manufactured perfection, and I was paralyzed to prevent it, nor did I want it to stop.

"Ahem… Ahem…" Shavonne pretended to clear her throat, which caused us to reluctantly break from each other's hold and look at her. "You better take good care of my girl." She threatened him.

He laughed, then looked back at me, "Don't worry. She's in good hands."

I grabbed my things as he took my hand into his and led me outside to where a black Maserati was parked. I couldn't help but marvel at the beast it was.

"Nice," I said, admiring the black rims and sleek finish.

He didn't respond with anything. He led me to the passenger side to open the door for me. I thanked him and got in. I watched his sexy frame in the rearview mirror as he walked around to the driver side, all the while thinking to myself the things I'd like to do with him and to his body.

He got into the driver's seat, and we were on our way. The only thing heard for the next few minutes were the sounds of Tank "Fucking with Me" playing softly in the background. This was not a good start to our date.

I was quiet because of my curiosity. I knew if I spoke, I would say something probably offensive, but why was he so quiet? I admired the car for a while longer—peanut-butter seats, wood-grain interior, state-of-the-art radio, etc. Then finally, unable to contain myself, I came out and asked what was on my mind.

Turning in my seat to face him, I asked, "Okay, spill it… what's the deal?"

He looked at me and asked, "What's the deal with what, gorgeous?"

"Yesterday, you were in a Bentley, and now it's this clean-ass Maserati, which looks brand new," I said to him. "Did you steal it?" I asked foolishly.

Instead of getting mad or offended, he laughed and said, "No. I didn't steal it."

"What? You borrowed it?" I pressed when he didn't say anything else.

In a humble tone, he looked over at me and said, "No… not borrowed either. I own a small dealership that sells and rents exotic cars here in Miami, along with a few clubs. I'm a businessman, baby, not a thief," he responded.

I was speechless. I wasn't expecting that. I was embarrassed for not thinking of him like that, instead going straight to the negative. I didn't know what to say or how I should say I was sorry, so I just turned back around and listened to the soft music playing through the speakers and let my mind drift into his words.

After a couple minutes of silence, I couldn't take it anymore. In an attempt to salvage the date, I mustered up the courage and said, "I'm sorry. I didn't mean to—"

"That's sexy as hell," he said out of nowhere, cutting me off.

Although I didn't know what he was referring to, I blushed. "What is?" I asked.

We arrived at an establishment that I thought was a small, country diner. It was brown with no sign and too remote to be a restaurant. Still not answering me, he got out of the car. *Rude ass*, I thought to myself. He made his way to the passenger side, opened the door for me, and offered me his hand.

I accepted it, and he helped me out, then said, "Your accent. It's sexy."

"Thank you," I said. "I was born in New York, lived there until I was about three when we moved here to Miami, and this has been home ever since." I quickly added. He just looked at me and smiled.

We walked into the establishment, and to my surprise, it was a restaurant. Right over the bar, there was the sign. It read *Sandra's Palace*. The inside was completely empty except for one table that was setup with two lit candles flickering to the wisp of air blowing from the open glass doors behind the bar revealing the night sky. It was beautiful. Also, on the table were petals of a rose that laid about delicately. He was watching me and smiled at the fact that I was in awe as I stood in place admiring the magnificent setting before me. We walked over to the table hand in hand. He sat me across from him, which I liked because occasionally, I could direct my legs to brush against his as a way to flirt using my body.

Dinner consisted of a lot of flirting, subtle touches, and laughter. We ate the best curry goat I'd ever tasted, red beans and rice, cabbage, corn bread, and salad. The Rhum de Melasse we were partaking in was giving me a buzz that was heightening my senses. Every time Malachi would brush his hand on top of mine or rub his leg across my thigh, I could feel it between my legs. We talked for what felt like hours and enjoyed each other's company. The more he talked, telling me about himself, the more I was feeling his vibe. He seemed impressed when I told him I owned my own event-planning company.

As we were being served dessert, rum cake, by the chef who was a business partner of his, I could hear festive music playing. Where it was coming, from I didn't know. I'm not sure if it was the buzz from the liquor and cake or what, but I perked myself up to listen and then began to sway my head, my hands, then my whole body to the sound of the music penetrating through the walls. Malachi watched me, smirking at me as my movements intensified as I was getting deeper into the music.

In the middle of my chair, winding and twerking, he grabbed my hand and asked, "You want to check it out?" I looked up at him. *When did he get up,* I thought.

"I absolutely do!" I said, enthused and ready to show my dancing skills.

He led me to the tiki bar behind the restaurant where the music was being played. The aroma of Caribbean food was flowing through the air. It was a beautiful atmosphere.

"So this is where everyone is hiding out? I was wondering where the other staff was," I said. "They didn't have to hide," I said.

"Not hiding, just staying out of our way. I wanted you to myself tonight," he replied.

I just smiled and nodded my head. This music was making my body move on its own. It was just that vibrant. Out of nowhere, Malachi pulled me into his body and began dancing on me closely. He must've been surprised I hadn't resisted. He pulled back and looked down at me. When he pulled me by the hips closer to him, I could feel a hard-on starting to manifest, but I continued dancing, rocking my backside on him in an erotic manner as if we were naked and joined together. When Rihanna's "Rude Boy" came on, I turned around to face him and sang the entire song as I continued my seductive dance on him.

He bent down and whispered in my ear, "You keep doing that, you'll find out how rude this boy is… trust me, baby. I'm more than big enough, but the question is, can you take it?" He then licked my ear. He gave me a slow grind so I could feel exactly how hard he was.

I looked up at him from beneath my lashes with a sexy, confident expression on my face and said, "I can handle all of you… I ain't worried 'bout nothing."

Yeah, I was definitely feeling the Rhum. I caressed the back of his neck, pulled him into me and kissed him like he was mine… full of passion. When we eventually pulled back and looked into each other's eyes, words were not needed. We both knew it was time to go before he ripped off my clothes on the dance floor.

"Let's get out of here," he groaned as his erection hardened more by my show of confidence. We said our goodbyes and headed back to the car.

Once in the car, I couldn't hold back my desperation of wanting him. I climbed over the middle console and straddled his lap, taking another kiss from his lips while I started slow grinding in his lap. My dress raised up around my hips to reveal a pair of black, lace panties. He looked down between my thighs and smirked.

His lips sought mine out again, and he kissed me slowly, taking his time memorizing my taste, and then he began nibbling on my bottom lip. "Damn, baby, you feel good," he said.

He reached over, removed my jacket, then begin to slide the straps of my dress down near my collarbone, but instead of pushing it completely down and off my shoulders, as I thought he would, he ran his finger slowly along the upper edge of my strapless lace bra in front and then traced it all the way around my breasts. I watched his face while he did this. It seemed more intimate, and I was burning with heat everywhere his hand touched.

By the time he'd finished outlining the whole thing, he'd barely touched my skin, yet I was so wet I could feel it through my panties. I continued to slowly move back and forth, grinding on his hard cock through his pants. My heartbeat accelerated. As every point in my body sparked with desire, I arched my back. My mouth opened as he started kissing and nibbling on my neck. I lost all control of my senses and leaned too far back, causing the horn of the car to go off, startling us to a halt.

Heaving and out of breath, we both looked at each other, neither wanting to stop. His hardened cock was throbbing against my soaking-wet sex. Reluctantly, I removed myself from his lap. Looking down in his lap, I noticed there was a small wet spot from where I'd sat on him. I fixed my dress and straightened out my hair best I could.

"I hope those aren't expensive," I said.

"It don't matter. I'm never washing your scent from them," he replied in a serious tone.

"You nasty." I sassed.

"You ain't even touched the surface of how nasty I can be, baby."

I sat there with my mouth open, not a slick remark in sight, which was a first for me. Malachi cranked his car, and we drove off… in complete silence.

CHAPTER 7

We arrived back to Shavonne's place in record time. The silence between us was beyond awkward. The heat that was between us was still palpable. We sat in the car a little while longer, trying desperately to engage in small talk, but the mood was not right for it. Neither one of us wanted the night to end. The lust we both were feeling needed an outlet.

He looked at his watch and saw how late it'd become and said jokingly, "I don't want your girl to beat me up. Let me get you inside." He got out of the car and came to my side to open the door for me. Hand in hand, we started to walk toward the door.

"Oh! So you scared of my friend, huh? Not big, bad Malachi!" I attempted to tease him, but in the moment, what I really wanted to do was protest and tell him how grown of a woman I was, but he seemed like he needed to leave.

Inside the condo hallway, Malachi let go of my hand as we reached the door. As I turned to face him, hoping for a kiss, he said, leaning against the opposite wall, "I really wish I could come in and spend some more time with you like you want me to, but I have to take a trip real early in the morning."

What the hell! I thought to myself and looked at him like he had inside information on me. Who told him I wanted to invite him in?

"Who said I wanted to ask you in?" I said firmly, not giving in to my desires to throw him against the wall and give him a reason to change his plans.

He looked at me with a smirk on his sexy ass lips like he could tell I was bullshitting. He stepped forward closer to me and lifted my chin up with his long index finger. My eyes fell to his lips. He tilted his head close to my lips and paused for a brief moment, no longer able to restrain himself. He leaned down and kissed me softly on the lips. He used his tongue to spread my lips apart. For a fleeting moment, we lingered there, inhaling against each other's partially-open mouths, breathing each other's air. The pulse-pounding rush of sensation that was trapped in my body seemed to have found its route of escape.

His tongue traced my lips, then dove in to tangle with mine. I swayed a little under the gust of heat. I wrapped my arms around his neck to steady myself, aligning our bodies so that more of us was touching than not. The closeness of our bodies gave me the opportunity to feel all of those delicious muscles that looked like they were screaming to be freed from under his shirt. With no choice but to act on my desperate impulse, I move my hand down his body to rest it on his chest, slowly letting it drift down to his abs, where he stopped it on his belt buckle.

Breaking our kiss, he stared into my eyes. When he saw that I was not going to move my hand, he returned his lips onto mine, allowing my hand to drift further down. The graveled sound that escaped him was enough to send a tremor directly to my sex just by the hot thread of desperation coming from his throat. Showing his desperation for me, just as I was for him, caused a soft moan to come out of me. I mused to myself how willpower had no place here as my legs started to buckle from the mounting pressure. Slowing the kiss so I could compose myself somewhat, I let my palm smooth over the bulging fly of his pants.

"Damn, it's big."

He laughed, and that was when I realized I said it out loud. I dropped my head. *Oh my goodness! I can't believe I said that out loud,* I said to myself

Still smiling, he said, "While you're lying in bed tonight, think about this."

My eyes jumped up to his as he slipped his big hands down the sides of my dress and around my waist to cup my mostly-bare ass. I had no time to enjoy the kick of lust in my belly before he seized my flesh tightly and hauled me onto my toes.

"Oh!" I gasped.

He placed his mouth directly over mine as if to absorb my gasp of shock as he said, "The first time you ride me, I'm going to grip your ass just like this." He tightened his hold on me. "I'm going to move you where I want you... how fast... how slow... it'll all be up to me and this grip." He finished.

Oh, God! Oh, God! I thought loudly in my head, his promise was filled with arrogance and assurance. It had me spinning into a frenzy, and I didn't have any idea how to control it. Every nerve in my body buzzed and hummed in anticipation and *Please... take me now.* The words seemed to scream through my mind.

"S-Sounds like a solid plan," I stuttered as I tried to catch my breath.

"Not a plan. A promise," he stated definitively and licked my mouth, kissing me in a way that promised—well, everything and more.

When he set me back on my feet, I felt wobbly in the knees.

"Goodnight, gorgeous," he said, then began to walk away, leaving me to drench in the river pool of wetness that was running down my thighs.

I felt stranded. Midway down to the elevator, away from me and the walls of Shavonne's condo that could be a victim to our category 5 heat of passion, I watched as he paused as if he had an epiphany. He looked at his watch again and abruptly turned and began heading back toward me. His strides were long and hurried as if he'd forgot something he needed. *Me,* I thought and hoped.

Hands sweating in anticipation. Chest rising and falling rapidly, accelerating beyond control as the heat of wanting labor my breathing. He reached me, and my pulse raced, our eyes ignited in flames of sensual translation as our body begins to speak foreign tongues. Unable to withhold the restraints of sexual desire, he pulled me into his arms and fondled my lips with his own.

My pulsing, heat-filled, beating heart felt as though it would stop. We momentarily broke free of each other's sensual grasp and gazed into each other's eyes with intense yearning. Searching for words that need not be spoken. The raw sweetness of his absent lips left me craving for some more. So I threw myself on him and ravished him hungrily. His hands effortlessly tranced down the contours of my body, pausing on my ass, and gently drew me even closer to him. Our bodies connected at the hips all the up to our heaving chests. Only our clothes kept our fire from spreading.

With my ass cupped in his hands, he lifted me up off the ground. I threw my legs around him, feeling his hard cock rubbing against my very-wet sex. He walked me in the house, pressed me against the closed door as we fumbled to tear each other's clothes off while he was carrying me into the room he'd saw me come out of earlier. All the while, I groped for him as though I were blind.

"Malachi, please, please," I moaned in a hoarse, unearthly voice.

My lips touched his, and we were kissing sloppily again. Slipping the now heavily-drenched dress over my head, his strong and gentle hands began to stroke me… his hands, his lips, his tongue. I was on fire. Somebody needed to call the firehouse because this building was about to go up in flames. His touch was gentle, not frightening. He knew exactly what he was doing. I felt my nipples rise to a hardened point, and it startled me to a moan.

"Shhh," he whispered. "Shhh, it's alright. Don't worry. Just relax and listen to your body." His touches moved along my body, slowly, rhythmically, and gently penetrating my skin with kisses as he moved his way further down.

Kissing and licking around my navel, I arched my back, pushing my body closer to his warm, wet mouth. His hands trailed up my naked torso, cupping each breast and rubbing my hardened nipples between his fingers and under the pad of his large hands. My back arched more my back now almost completely off the bed seeking more of him… of his touch.

When his hands moved back down, I whimpered at the loss of contact until I felt his body shift, and then his hot, wet tongue started to tease and suck each breast in turn. A flame coiled in my belly, causing an ache that only he could soothe right now. I tried to move my hands, but he has them pinned above my head. My disappointment in not being able to touch was quickly wiped away when he moved his head back further down, licking my sensitive flesh. I could feel his tongue dip into my navel, and I squirmed, eager for him to keep going. He chuckled, and the sound of his deep voice traveled to where I was starving for him.

"A little greedy are we?" He breathed onto my flesh. His hands stopped at my hips, and he used his knee to nudge my thighs further apart, exposing me to him completely. "Look at me," he commanded. "I want you to watch me use my tongue to make you cum." I shivered, and out of reflex, my eyes closed. "Passion," he growled.

My eyes snapped open, and I look into his mocha-brown eyes. A storm of lust and hunger swirled viciously in their depths. He licked his lips, and a moan slipped from between my slightly-parted lips.

"Oh… please!" I begged, unable to help myself.

He was driving me so wild, and I was being consumed by my own ravenous need. I wanted him to own me, consume me, and give me what I craved. *Him.* He kissed my inner thigh on my left side, and then he kissed the right, his piercing gaze never leaving mine.

"Please what, baby?" He teased, looking up at me from between my legs.

He wanted me to tell him what I wanted from him… to fuck me. The wicked grin on his face made me feel like a helpless rabbit about to be devoured by a wolf… a big, bad wolf.

He leaned down, and I heard him inhale my scent. "Hmmm," he mumbled. "Sweet as a ripe Georgia peach." I watched as he lifted my legs and wrapped them around his neck. My heart was already racing, but by some miracle, it increased in speed. "Tell me what you want," he demanded again. I licked my dry lips and force the words out from my very dry mouth.

"I want you to fuck me with your tongue… Please!"

He grinned wickedly. My big, bad wolf. His eyes stay glued to mine as his head dipped, and I held my breath in anticipation. His tongue dove between my slick folds. The heat and moisture assaulted my clit. My hips buckled, and I felt him smile against me. He teased me, pushing me upon the edge within reach of an orgasm, then pulled back, keeping me on the edge of the cliff. His tongue slid between my sensitive lips until it reached the little hub of nerves he was searching for. The familiar pressure built, and when I thought I was ready to crash, his mouth pulled back again.

I struggled to catch my breath, panting loudly. Suddenly, I felt his mouth covering mine. I could taste myself on him, which only served to increase my arousal.

"Please!" I breathed into his mouth. "I don't think I can—" My words were cut off when he slowly slipped one finger into me and then another.

Then started the beginning of his slow, torturous process of teasing my clit all over again. My hips started moving and fell into rhythm with his fingers while I rode his hand.

"Yes." I breathed harshly "Oh my God! Yes!"

He started curling his fingers upward, massaging my upper walls, searching for my G-spot. Each time his fingers retreated, he applied more pressure as they surged back in. I couldn't help but think that he was a musician, and I was the instrument. The wave of ecstasy was close, and I felt myself tighten around his fingers until...

The front door opened, and I heard the voice of a stranger enter. I sat straight up on the bed, and then I heard the laughter of Shavonne.

"Passion, you in?" she called out.

I didn't want to respond mainly because I've lost my voice, thanks to the big, bad wolf that was Malachi, but I cleared my throat and managed to say, "Yeah!" with a whine in my voice.

"How was your date?" I heard her ask. However, my focus was back on Malachi as he moved from the bed and started removing his clothes. Goodness! This man's body should be illegal.

"It's still going on," I said with a gasp and left it that, completely tuning her out.

Malachi grabbed me by the ankle, pulling me closer to the edge of the bed and flipped me over, face-first onto the bed. He ran his hands along the side of my body, slowly and meticulously, as if I was an intricate piece of art for his studying. Then he abruptly pulled me back toward him by my hips, causing a soft moan to flee between my lips. He lifted my ass slightly off the bed, and with one of his hands placed at the small of my back, he raised up the other and smacked my ass. Cupping a handful of it at the same time.

Smack!

"Oh," I moaned, panting as I felt my breath leaving my body. It stung, but the sensation that jolted through my body was unexplainable. The beating of my heart sped up, leaving my lungs to grasp for absent air. He raised up his hand again, and with and equal amount of power and force, brought it down on my ass.

Smack!

"Oh, God!" I moaned, feeling my mind drifting into the abyss of erotic sensation.

With his body pressed against mine, he leaned toward my ears and whispered, "Passion, I'm gon' make you feel real good, ma."

Shit... hurry up! I thought to myself as foreign pleasures invade my senses with bodily heat, causing tremors to take flight between my thighs. I heard the wrapper of the condom being torn. I arched my back more, silently telling him with my body to hurry up. There was a brief, sharp pain as he entered me slowly, followed by a sweet shiver that flowed up my spine.

I immediately felt an orgasm mounting. But I somehow, for whatever unknown reason, got the urge to ask him if I could cum. He started caressing my neck with kisses. I welcomed it with a moan and moved my head slightly for him to work his magic as I reached back and rubbed my hand on the back of his neck. My upper thighs began to quiver, and my muscles tighten in my stomach I feel my head began to spin, uncontrollably. I felt like I was on the cliff of a volcano that was about to erupt.

He must've felt that I was cumming too because he interlocked his finger onto mine and whispered, "Don't cum yet… I have a lot more to give you."

What the fuck? I thought to myself as wave of hot and calm sensations washed over me. Pulling out of me, he flipped me over and put me on the bottom. My legs got placed in the bends of his arms. He went back in with one thrust… I could feel him deep… real deep.

He put my right breast in his mouth, then started to suck and nibble on it as he pinched, squeezed, massaged, and pulled at the left nipple ring, never stopping the music he's making with his hips. It was torture, but fuck it felt so good—pain and pleasure. Jolts of multiple hedonisms started zapping from the very tip of my fingers all the way to the back of my knees, weakening me. The feeling was unbearable to withstand. I felt like a compressed fire burning ablaze. At the slightest crack of air, I was gonna burst.

He placed his big, strong arms under me again, lifting and rolling us over, putting me on top while still inside of me. That's when it happened. It felt like every inch of him was hitting my G-spot. I lost awareness in the throes of his deep strokes. Leaning my head back, I started grinding on his cock. I rode slow, momentarily picking up a faster pace with purpose like I was riding a thoroughbred stallion.

He was holding on to my waist, leaving his finger imprints in my skin, and then he groaned, "Fuck. You better ride this dick." His words made me wetter. My breathing becomes faster and more irregular. My pussy began to pulse, gripping tighter to his dick.

A giant flood of my wetness left my body, and I exploded, squirting all over his cock while moaning his name, "Malachi." I felt an instant release from the fullness I was carrying. I grabbed tightly to his chest as my body gradually stopped all my movement.

He seemed to enjoy watching me shake and shiver. His body continued to thrust upward into me, never breaking stride, moving even deeper, going harder than he already was. I whimpered my satisfaction. As his pace continued to pick up, I started to move with him. His grip tightened on my hips, and with a grunt, his body stilled as he came into the condom.

Panting and groaning as we both tried catching our breath, our eyes met. He lifted up slightly and kissed me softly on my lips and neck. I smiled. He winked. I briefly closed my eyes, exhaled, then I collapse beside him, unable to move, think, or speak. Every ounce of energy had been sucked out of me.

But I wanted more. I was just too drained to get up. I felt him lift from the bed and heard him walk into the bathroom to flush the condom. I fell asleep on him, completely naked and sprawled out in bed. Last thing I remembered was him coming into the room with a washcloth and cleaning me up. After that, I was lights out.

CHAPTER 8

It's not the invigorating breeze that was sweeping throughout the room that woke me up. Nor was it the memories of the mind-blowing rendezvous of sex I had last night that kept playing in my dreams. Instead, it's the welcoming aroma of delicious Caribbean food invading my nostrils. I lay still under the plush sheets that were wrapping only half of my body, while taking in all in the smells.

When my stomach growled, I smiled, blushing to myself. The smell had me reminiscing the thrill from last night's roller-coaster ride or that's what it felt like. Images of him on top of me, behind me, below me as I rode began to fill my mind. I satisfyingly bit my bottom lip, opened my eyes, and turned my head to the side only to find, to my dismay, that the other side of the bed was empty. I was filled with disappointment.

Soon as I lifted my body to get up and get out of bed, the room door opened, and there he was standing there, looking like a magnificent sculpture carved by the female gods themselves— Malachi. In his hands was what woke me up from my slumber, a tray of some good-smelling breakfast.

I sat up in awe and smiled at him. He smiled back. I could also see the lust and need in his eyes. I was sure mine were reflecting the same. He licked his lips and flexed his chest muscle at me. I felt a thunderous pulse shoot between my thighs and run up my spine.

"Good morning, beautiful," he said to me, walking toward me with the tray of food, "I ordered you some breakfast from where we ate last night," he announced. "Are you hungry?" His voice was so deep and enchanting with his southern accent. It resonated throughout the inner parts of my being once again. I want him again. *Badly*.

"Good morning to you too, sir! Thank you! That was very considerate of you to think of me and my belly this morning," I said appreciatively in a husky, dreamy voice as he placed the tray filled with good-smelling food across my lap.

In all my years, I'd never had a man, besides Khalil, bring me breakfast in bed. Looking at me with eyes of utter admiration and affection, he smirked. We were both sitting in bliss gleaming with fondness. His eyes quickly found mine, making me feel as though I was the only star that adorned his sky. I could feel my temperature rising with want again.

My body called out to him as he sat beside me on the bed, looking glorious and enticing. I ran my hand along the length of his smooth, chocolate, muscular arms as I pulled him down to kiss me. The kiss started off slow and sensual. I moved my hand downward and placed my hand on the crotch of his pants. I started stroking and stimulating his already-bulging cock. He groaned, letting me know he liked what I was doing.

"Hmmmmm." I let out a light moan too as he reached down and started to caress my bare sex with his fingers. My phone started to ring, disrupting our moment of simmering heat. I quickly looked over at it to see none other than Khalil's name. I turn back to Malachi and simply ignored it.

He pulled back, looked at me, and asked, "Do you want to answer that?" His beautiful, erect cock was now out of his pants, staring right at me. It was a dart, and my eyes, being so focused on it, made it like a bullseye.

My phone was the last thing on my mind right now. I shook my head no while pulling his face toward me and his lips back on mine. His fingers started back massaging my love box with even more determination. It felt exhilarating as the sensations heightened my arousal. I ignored the constant ringing of my phone, pulled him closer to me, and kept his lips on mine. His fingers began to establish its rhythm again, going in and out very methodically, getting me wetter by the second.

My phone rang again. *Ugghhh!*

Immediately, I tried to turn it off, but that wasn't what happened. In my attempt to turn the ringing phone off, I accidentally knocked it off the nightstand and onto the floor. Not my intention, but it stopped ringing.

Again, I pulled his face back to mine and kissed him… fervently. I kissed him as though this was the last time I'd get to kiss him again. The last time I'd get to see or feel him again. He kissed me back with equal urgency and desire. The smooth crashing and ebbing of the ocean waves in the background carried its calming ambience into the room. The drapes danced in the harmony of added movement around us.

I felt myself being pulled in a whirling frenzy, ready to embark on a repeat of our sexcape done last night when there comes a knock at the door. **Knock! Knock!** We both stop and looked toward the door to the room. *I wonder who that can be. Shavonne ain't no blocker.*

"What!" I yelled frustrated.

"So we ignoring calls now?"

Instantly, I stopped breathing when I heard Khalil's voice.

"Who the fuck is that?" asked Malachi.

"Umm… nobody," I said in a daze at a loss for words. Never would I have imagined it to be Khalil knocking at the door.

Knock! Knock!

"Ajah, what the fuck, man! You alright in there?" Khalil asked with anger obvious in his voice.

"Who is Ajah?" Malachi asked with a frown on his face. *Fuck!*

"Khalil, give me a minute. I have company!" I yell at the door.

Malachi starts to get up and dressed.

"Malachi, wait. That's just my best friend," I anxiously stated. "I didn't know he was in town," I explained.

"You good, ma. Handle yo' business," he said with extra, added bass in his voice. "I'll holla at you later."

"Malachi, wait. He's just joking. We're a protective crew, but he's not my man," I said, trying to convince him to chill so we could finish what we started. My pussy was throbbing, and I was horny. Khalil's ass could wait.

"Oh, I ain't worried, ma, but I should get going. I have business to handle," he replied, now completed dressed.

"We have unfinished business here, Malachi," I said with a whine.

He chuckled. "Naw. I'll call you later." With that, he gave me an impassive kiss on my lips, all the sweetness gone from the moment, and walked toward the door.

"Malachi!" I call out to him.

"Yeah?" he asked with his back still to me.

"Talk to you later?" I asked.

"I got you, ma," he said, looking over his shoulder with a smirk, and then he was out the bedroom door.

Before the door could fully close, I heard Khalil ask, "Hey, who you?" His voice full of anger.

I jump out of bed, throw on Malachi's T-shirt laying on the floor, and run toward the front door.

"Ask *Ajah*, bruh. Don't fucking question me," Malachi replied with a mean mug on his handsome face.

"Nigga, you got me fucked up. I question who the fuck I want when it comes to Ajah. Easiest way to lose yo' life is fucking off with that one," Khalil said while walking toward Malachi.

I saw Malachi reach for his waist. I rushed to step in between them.

"Hey… Hey! Stop! Khalil, stop please!" I said in an aggravated, whiny, yelling tone. "Malachi, I apologize. Come on, let me walk you out," I said as calmly as I could, looking between them, trying to get Malachi to walk toward the door, but he wasn't bulging. Instead, they continued to have a stare down. Malachi's hand still near his waist. To my relief, Shavonne walked into the foyer, where we were standing, and pulled Khalil reluctantly toward the kitchen.

"Malachi… please," I pleaded. He looked down at me pulled away from my grasp, walking backward to the door, and he walked out the front door without saying another word. I dropped my head. *Damn, Khalil!*

I walked into the kitchen furiously. Khalil had the nerve to be mean mugging me like I did something wrong to him

"Really, Khalil!" I said. "How dare you? I am not Destiny! You can't be acting like the jealous boyfriend when it comes to me. You trying to make me single forever! Dang! Ugh!" He got me all the way fucked up.

"Miss me with all that bullshit. What kind of guys you picking up out here? If it wasn't for you stepping in, I would've broken his neck before his soft ass would have reached his gun," Khalil said with obvious anger in his tone. "You know how I am, Ajah. Don't act like you don't. You better get your playthings in check," he said, looking me straight in my eyes.

I was in shock. Khalil was really tripping right now. I couldn't take his face right now. I was so mad at him and this entire unnecessary situation, so I just walked back toward the room. I needed to indulge in a hot bath to relax and meditate. This was too much drama too early in the morning. Although I was happy to see Khalil, I wished he would've stayed in Texas. He fucked up my morning orgasm. Now I was forced to masturbate in the bath to take off this edge I was left with.

CHAPTER 9

Knock! Knock!

Before I answered, the door opened.

"Man, come on out of here being a brat. Let's go to the beach," Shavonne said as she walked into the bedroom. I should've known it was her. She refused to ask for permission to enter.

"Girl… why yo' friend come in here cockblocking early in the morning?" I replied with a laugh.

"'Cause… nah, never mind. I'ma keep my mouth closed on this one. Anyway, get dressed so we can go!" she yelled over her shoulder, heading for the door again, not waiting on a response from me. "Demanding self," I mumbled.

With that, I just rolled my eyes and headed into the wardrobe to pull my swimsuit from my duffle bag. Once on the beach, we were joined by a few of Shavonne's friends—some are familiar, others are not, but they're all fun just like my girl. The sun is brightly illuminating the skies, taking with it the drama from this morning, something my bubble bath from earlier had failed to completely do. I just wanted to dip my feet in this beautiful saltwater, take a few selfies, and have enough drinks to not be horny when I got back to Shavonne's place…alone.

"You still mad at me?" I looked up to see Khalil standing next to me as I sat near the shore watching the waves.

"Nah… you know I can't stay mad at you too long, even when you deserve it," I replied with a chuckle.

"Good. Because I didn't want to have to hurt you," he said as he sat down beside me. "So what's up with you and dude from this morning?" he asked.

"Nothing, Khalil… I don't want to talk about that with you," I said with a groan, really not wanting to recap the drama by having this conversation with him.

"Since when we keep secrets?" he asked with a frown on his handsome face. He made me so sick.

"It's not a secret. It's just… ugh… I don't want to think about none of that. I just want to enjoy the rest of my vacation, drama free," I said with a pleading undertone.

"Alright, I can give you that," was all he said in return, somewhat dropping the subject. Thank goodness.

"What you doing in Miami anyway?" I asked him.

"I got called to Tampa to see about one of my patients and decided to stop here instead of going back home. Is that a problem?" He angled his head to the side and got closer in my face with his eyebrow raised. Frequent travel was not an unusual occurrence with Khalil and his job, being that he was one of the most sought-after sports medicine physicians in the country.

"Little lonely without your boo?" I asked laughing.

"Hell no! Trying to get away from that crazy girl and her latest bullshit," he said, shaking his head "Plus, I was missing you," he said.

I looked up expecting a playful smile to be on his face. Instead, I was met with intense, unwavering eye contact. *What the fuck is going on with Khalil lately?* I thought. I turned back to the water and let the waves take over my thoughts because I was at a loss for words. After sitting together in silence for about twenty minutes, Khalil and I joined Shavonne back up the beach at the picnic area.

"Y'all good?" Shavonne asked us as soon as we got close to her.

"You know we're always going to be good. Ajah can't get away from me. I won't let her," Khalil responded. I just shook my head.

"Sha, why Khalil think he got it like that? Don't he know I'll drop him like a bad habit?" I said, laughing. Shavonne just sucked her teeth and shook her head. "What! Shavonne, for real? You gonna do me like that?" I look at her with a frown.

"I love you, Passion, but we both know Khalil is telling the truth," she replied all serious.

"Well, dammit. I guess the jokes on me then." I fake a pout.

Khalil burst out laughing, then kissed me on the cheek and walked over to the grill to make us something to eat. We spent the rest of the night laughing, drinking, and enjoying the beautiful weather of Miami with Shavonne and her crew. Kaysha's "Malembe Malembe" played in the background while Khalil and I showed off our kizomba skills. We thought we were professionals after we took a class last year after attending one of his colleagues wedding. We became intrigued after the loving couple performed it as their first dance, so of course, we had to learn the dance in its entirety, and we always enjoyed showing off what we learned.

As the sun set and everyone else left, Khalil, Shavonne, and I walked along the strip, talking until three in the morning. We even dipped into a few bars and smoked a couple of Cuban cigars.

I was in heaven... this was what a vacation was... living, loving, laughing with my two best friends.

✳✳✳

I hadn't heard from Malachi since the morning he left. After the altercation with Khalil, I texted him. Even called, but I guess he got what he wanted from me, and he was good on me now. I wasn't tripping though, because I got what I wanted as well, and I was copacetic. Khalil, Shavonne, and I spent the next day, after partying on the beach, with our parents at my parents' restaurant in Fort Lauderdale. We ate lobster mac and cheese while visiting and getting grilled about us all being single. Shavonne's parents also joined us.

Two beautiful days later, Khalil and I flew back to Texas on his private jet. I loved flying private. First-class seats could not compare to the luxury and peace of it. While in flight, Khalil received a work call, so he stayed aboard after we landed and headed to Houston after refueling. One of his Houston Texan players reinjured his ankle after partying with his friends while on South Padre Island. I guess that's the doctor life for ya. Although he asked me to tag along, I stayed behind because I had work to do, and I was fine with that. I was vacationed out at this point and ready to get back to the money.

Later on that night I went out to get me something to eat. I was craving pasta, so I went for something simple—Olive Garden. Sitting occupied at the bar, waiting for my takeout, I heard this woman giggling, being all loud and obnoxious. When I looked up from my phone to be nosy, to my surprise, I saw Destiny all hugged up with some sexy ass, chocolate man. I sneakily took a couple pictures with my phone and sent them to Khalil. Immediately, he texted back.

Khalil: Good. Maybe now she'll stop calling me fake crying. LOL!

Me: Nah… I'm sure she'll still stalk you. LOL!

Khalil: Where are you?

*Me: Olive Garden, getting me some pasta! *tongue sticking out emoji**

*Khalil: Without me? *sad emoji**

Me: Ummm… you are in Houston, sir, and I am hungry… so yeah, without you. LOL!

Khalil: I told you to come with me to Houston, but you were soooo busy… not too busy for Olive Garden tho, huh?

Me: I have work to do still, Khalil. It's all good. It's takeout anyway. A girl still has to eat right?

Khalil: Whatever… I gotta go I'll see you TMW.

Me: Okay… love ya, bestie. Nighty-night.

Khalil: Good night.

For the life of me, I couldn't understand this new mood Khalil has been in with me. When he got home, we were going to have a really good conversation, I could live without a lot of people, but Khalil wasn't one of them.

With that thought, I got my food and headed to the home I shared with Khalil… alone with only my mind as company—just how my overthinking self needed it to be right now.

Malachi still did not contact me, and I was counting that L for what it was. After getting home, I took a hot shower, talked to Shavonne on the phone, and went to bed relaxed and full. Guess I'll do some work tomorrow. For now, I'm gonna enjoy this quiet.

CHAPTER 10

Boom! Boom!

What the—it's three a.m. Who could this be?

Boom! Boom! Boom!

"Who is it!" I yell, walking toward the door with my gun in my hand.

Boom! Boom!

I looked at the security app on my phone as I walk toward the door. "How did this girl get through the guard? She must be fucking him too," I mumbled to myself.

Stopping at the bottom of the stairs and sitting on the second from the last, I texted Khalil. I didn't care how late it was. This was his problem, not mine.

Me: *Your stalker is here, and I'm ten seconds away from calling the coroner for her and the gate guard!*

Instantaneously, I hear Destiny's phone ringing, and I know it's Khalil. "Hello?" I can hear Destiny answering her phone. She's so loud that it sounds like she is in the house with me. "Khalil, I refuse… No… No! Come outside! She's lying, Khalil!" I heard her whimpering, then sniffling, followed by loud cries. "I hate her, Khalil… whatever… okay. I'm leaving." She stuck her middle finger up at the camera by the door and stormed off to her car. All I heard after that is the screeching of her tires out of the driveway and my phone pinging a notification of a new text message. I almost ignored it just to piss him off 'cause I'm enraged, but I check it despite myself.

48

Khalil: *I am so sorry about that. She won't be coming back, and I'll make sure to have a talk with the gate company, not just the guard tomorrow… okay?*

Me: *I think I need to get my own spot. I'm not about to deal with this crap, Khalil…I refuse.*

Be my best friend.

Be my best friend, mmm.

Be my best friend, mmmm.

NBA Youngboy's "Best Friend" started playing in my hand. I dramatically exhaled because I already know who it was by the ringtone.

"Yes, Khalil?" I asked with an attitude.

"Don't do me like that. You are not allowed to move from our home," he replied, trying to lighten the mood.

"This is not funny, Khalil! If she's gonna be like this, I will leave. My sanity and safety are worth more than your ex-lover still trying to hold on," I said.

"Then we'll be moving together. I'll send Jordyn an email so she can start the process of looking for us a new house tomorrow," he said.

"Khalil, why do I have to live with yo—"

Cutting me off, he replied, "Because I want you to. Just relax. I got us. Look, I just left from work, and I fly out in three hours. I'll see you in the morning."

Did he really just cut me off and shut me up in the same sentence? "Maybe you will." I tried to gain back my wannabe dominant position.

"No! I will find you somebody else to play with. You know to not play with me, Ajah. I'll see you in the morning. Love ya. Good night."

"Good night, Khalil." I pouted, then hung up on him as he chuckled in my ear.

✳✳✳

I awakened later in the morning than usual in a dreamlike state to strong arms wrapped around my body. As a natural reflex I do the only thing that feels instinctive——I move my body closer into the hard body behind me. Immediately, I feel an erection pushed into my ass, and I begin to wind on it. In the state of mind I was in at that moment, morning sex was exactly the remedy I needed to relieve the stressful pressures in my head.

I heard a groan in my ear. As the arms around me tightened, I grinded harder. Then a hand was moving down my stomach, all the way between my legs. I moaned.

"Ahhh... mmm."

My panties are pulled to the side, and I feel a big finger enter me. I winded more and whimpered. I threw my head back, opened my eyes, and looked over my shoulder... it's Khalil. Instantly, I jump to the other side of the bed.

"Khalil! What the fuck!" I screamed.

"What?" he asked like he just didn't have his finger in me.

"What are you doing in bed with me?" I asked, pulling the covers up to my chin.

Tilting his head to the side, looking at me like I was crazy, he nonchalantly replies, "Sleeping." Yeah, he has lost his mind just like Destiny.

"With your fingers in me, Khalil? Really!"

His face changed into a half smirk, like he was trying not to smirk but couldn't help himself. "Okay, my bad it was a reflex. I woke up with you moaning and grinding on me, like... what do you expect my reaction to that to be?"

I just stared at him 'cause *really?* "Why did you get in the bed with me instead of going to your bed anyway?" I asked.

"I came in here to check on you when I got home, and you asked me to come lay with you, so I did." He shrugged.

"I don't remember that," I said with a groan.

"Listen, I'm sorry about touching you, but I don't regret it." Khalil's eyes and face changed right before my face. Now there's lust and desire staring back at me. I didn't acknowledge what he was saying to me. I just stared at him, puzzled. What does he mean he didn't regret it?

"Look, I want to talk to you about something. I have Jordyn looking for us a bigger place, and I want you to go with me to pick out our next home because you are not moving without me," he demanded.

"Khalil—" I started to say, but again like last night, he cut me off.

"No, listen, I've been thinking a lot lately. Thinking about us and what we could be beyond best friends." I couldn't speak. I just continued to look him in his eyes as he continued to talk. "I didn't perceive how much I needed to stop dragging my ass and go for what I really wanted until I realized that my opportunity to have you may not be an option anymore," he said without any credence.

"So you want me *now* because you saw me with someone else or because you're single?" I said with an attitude. How dare he act like I was a consolation prize?

"I never not wanted you, Ajah," he responded with so much sincerity. "You were my first kiss, the first time I made love was with you, and every goal I've conquered and achieved was with you by my side and contrariwise. How can you not know that you are my forever? I just felt like you deserved the chance to see what else was out there before I locked you down." There was no smile, no apprehension in his words. He meant everything he was telling me.

"Khalil, you are my best friend. I don't want to do anything to lose you. What happens when you realize it's too much?" I said with sass, really being petty so my true exhilaration of how much I wanted this too won't show.

"You don't want this, Ajah?" he asked, making a hand motion between us and speaking in a serious tone that let me know his feelings were real, and he wasn't playing.

"That's not what I'm saying, Khalil. Don't put words in my mouth. I'm saying that I'm scared, and as much as I may want to explore this too, I don't want this to be a mistake. I can't live without you in my life, Khalil," I said, not breaking eye contact. I meant business too.

"What are you saying then, Ajah?" he asked.

"I'm saying… I'm afraid of the risk this carries," I said, dropping my head and looking at my hands. He placed his fingers under my chin and lifted my eyes back to his.

"We can go as slow as you want to. Let's just take our time and explore each other as adults, no longer kids, and let what will be, progress," he said, raising his eyebrow in question.

Smiling, I replied, "You are so arrogant You just know this is gonna work!" I shook my head and chuckled.

"Without a doubt," he said full of confidence that only Khalil can possess.

"So we really gonna do this?" I asked, biting my bottom lip.

"Only if you want to." He countered.

"I want to." My smile was so big my face hurt, and my heart was beating so loud I'm almost sure he heard it.

"Grown Khalil is nothing like college Khalil. I know what I want." He paused, looked me directly in the eyes, then pointed between the two of us as he said, "This... us... Khalil and Ajah taking this step is everything that I have ever wanted. It's only going to make our bond stronger. Us being best friends just makes the chemistry and connection deeper. I'm going to make you so happy, baby." He leaned in and placed a kiss on my cheek, then my lips.

A shiver ran down my spine, and I blushed. "We'll see, Mr. Black," I replied, trying to place it off.

"Bet. Now can I get a real kiss to seal the deal, or better yet, we can finish what we started earlier?" he said with a smirk.

"Naw... you gotta earn those pleasures, but I *will* give you a peck," I said as I leaned a few inches closer to give him a kiss.

Our lips softly brush together. I pecked his lips, and they felt like marshmallows. They were so soft and full. Expeditiously, Khalil grabbed the back of my neck and deepened the kiss, adding his tongue. His other hand moves to my chin, pulling me closer, making me lean in more—knees touching, chests heaving up and down, hands roaming, mine more than his.

Then abruptly, I pulled away and looked him directly in his eyes and said, "God help me."

He just burst out laughing. I shook my head side to side and sent a silent request up above. *Please let this work 'cause if his kiss is this splendiferous, I can only imagine what else is in store for me.*

CHAPTER 11

Waking up to the smell of breakfast would always be one of my favorite things. Of course, morning sex is number one, but I loved the aroma of bacon and pancakes waking me up in the morning. It's pure joy to the phat girl in me.

Groaning, I rolled over to my left side to get out of bed and start my day. Instinctively, I rubbed my hand on the pillow in front of my face, then pulled it into me to smell it. It still smelled like him. I closed my eyes and inhaled. The smell brought back memories of the events of yesterday—the kiss I shared with Khalil, the talk we had as we lay facing each other laughing while reminiscing about the good ole days, Khalil reassuring me again that we got this so I needed to let go of my fears that our friendship will suffer by us becoming a couple, and the way my body responded to his touch as he rubbed his hand up and down my back while we talked for hours, blocking out everything else until he was called into work. His confidence and assurance in regard to us being a *we* made me more confident, and that shit turned me on.

Walking into my bathroom, I looked at myself in the mirror, "I'm dating my best friend," I said to my friend in the mirror looking back at me, and I must admit, even saying it out loud sounded perfectly weird.

I turned on the shower to let the water warm up and start my hygiene. After brushing my teeth and washing my face, I hopped in the shower. During my shower, I had a hard time keeping my mind off Khalil and my hands from my pussy, which turned my morning shower into a quick morning orgasm. Finishing one of the best showers I'd had in a while, I got dressed in something comfortable, because I only had plans to work from home today, then I headed down to the kitchen to see what was cooking. I knew I smelled bacon and pancakes, but I couldn't be sure.

When I walked into the kitchen, on the island are lilies—two huge, beautiful pink-and-white arrangements—and they immediately put a smile on my face. However, before I'm able to pick up the card sitting between the vases, a gorgeous, dark-chocolate woman with a mini afro, wide hips, and a slim waist walked into the house from the patio area. *Who is this?* I thought. When I opened my mouth to express this exact sentiment, she spoke up first.

"Buenos días, señora. (Good morning, madam.)" She greets me with this huge smile on her face.

"Buenos días. ¿Quién eres? (Good morning. Who are you?)" I definitely did not expect her to start speaking Spanish. *I will never judge a book by its cover again,* I thought to myself.

"Mi nombre es ZaNita. El Sr. Khalil me contrató para que preparara su desayuno esta mañana. ¿Qué te gustaría? (My name is ZaNita. Mr. Khalil hired me to prepare your breakfast this morning. What would you like?)" she replied, still with that big smile on her face.

I look her up and down, and then realized I completely missed the apron she was wearing. Only my Khalil, always the gentleman and charmer… did I just say *my* Khalil. Stay focused Ajah… relax.

"Tomaré una tortilla de bistec con salsa y unas piñas en rodajas al lado. Gracias! (I'll have a steak omelet with salsa and some sliced pineapples on the side. Thank you!)" I replied, finally returning her smile.

"De inmediato, señora, (Immediately, madam,)" she said, heading deeper into the kitchen where I saw a plate of cooked bacon and a carton of eggs sitting on the counter near the stove. She began preparing my breakfast.

"Puedes llamarme Ajah. Gracias, Sra. ZaNita. (You can call me Ajah. Thank you, Ms. ZaNita.)"

I grabbed the card from between the beautiful flowers and moved over to the table to read it. The card was so exquisite I almost didn't want to open it. The card was made of a cloth material with gold trim and a blush-colored writing—fancy. Opening up the card, I saw… a note written in Khalil's handwriting on the left side and a poem written on the right. *Since when did Khalil write poetry?* I thought with a frown on my face.

Good morning, my beautiful beginning! I wish I was there to personally cook your steak omelet, but duty calls. Enjoy ZaNita. She's a beast in the kitchen, almost as good as me. Here are a few words to carry you until we see each other later.
Yours Truly,
Big Daddy

Like the blossomed rose that harmonizes to a field of lilies,

You are the gentleness of a breeze that sways me into the threshold of blissfulness.
You're like the finery stroke of an artist's masterpiece,
The elegance in your eyes defines the frame that beholds the painting.
Your very touch travels the depth of me, melts unto my heart, and
Unravels my soul with the sensation of a sublime kiss….

You were looking too delectably delicious when I left this morning. Mmmm, mmm, mmm… I didn't want to wake you, so here's a gift to let you know that although we are not together, you are with me. I hope your day is enjoyable while you're in absence from me. :-* :-*

Until I lay my eyes upon you again,
One

I was in utter shock and awe, never have I known Khalil to write poetry. And how did he know what I was gonna order, like he knows me or something. What have I gotten myself into he is not holding any punches? I sent him a text, even though I wanted to call I knew that his clientele's privacy was everything, so I conceded.

Me: *Well… Good morning, smooth Casanova! Your gesture has captured my attention… thank you.*

His response was not hastened. I knew that was how it was going to be, especially with him being at work. However, the brat in me wanted him to answer me right away. Still with my phone in my hand, I begin going through emails and deleting messages. After fifteen minutes, I was approached by ZaNita.

"Su desayuno está listo, señora. (Your breakfast is ready, madam.)"

Didn't I ask her to call me Ajah? I turned around to see ZaNita holding the most delectable-looking omelet I've ever seen. She could call me madam all she wants. I hoped this taste as good as it looked.

"Gracias, ZaNita! Esto se ve delicioso. ¿Tienes zumo de naranja? (Thank you, ZaNita. This looks delicious. Do you have any orange juice?)" I asked her as she sat the plate in front of me at the table, along with a cutlery set… nice!

After she placed the orange juice beside my plate, she was out the door as fast as she came. My phone started ringing. I picked it up without looking to see who the caller was because my face was in my plate.

"Hello?" I recognized the deep, baritone voice, even if I had not heard it in close to a week. I knew exactly who the caller was. "Passion?" he said again.

I guess I didn't answer fast enough for him, but I couldn't because I froze up. For some reason, I wasn't sure if it was shock or what, but I could not find my voice.

After clearing my throat I finally responded, "Y-Yes?" I hated the stammer in my voice. *Ajah tighten up,* I coached myself mentally.

"What's up? It's Malachi," he said like he didn't ghost me, and we were cool.

"Malachi who?" I asked. Yeah, it was petty, but the bitch in me didn't care at this moment. Who did he think he was calling me like I was just sitting around waiting on him to return my calls and text messages?

"Damn, it's like that?" he said with a slight chuckle.

"You're the one ignoring calls and texts, making me feel like a stalker, then getting ghost… so yeah, it's like that," I replied with so much attitude.

"I'm sorry about that, ma. Shit got hectic over here on my end," Malachi responded.

"Yeah, whatever," was all I gave him back. He chuckled. *Bastard.*

"Can I make it up to you? I can be at your spot in thirty minutes."

Shit! Now he wanna pop back up, and how the hell he know where I lived? Maybe he thought I was still in Miami.

"I'm not in Miami right now," I said, trying to feel him out and see what he knew.

"Neither am I." This dude was crazy. Now who's the stalker?

"What!" I whispered, mostly to myself.

"I'm in Texas, and I can be to you in thirty, so what's good?"

Again, how did he know where I lived? I did not like the direction the conversation was going in. I never told Malachi my real name or where I actually lived. Did he go by Shavonne's house, and she told him? I'ma kill her. Just as I was about to respond to ask him how the hell he knew where I was, my phone notification beeped in my ear. Moving the phone from my ear, I noticed I had a text from Khalil.

Khalil: *Good morning, baby. I'm glad you're enjoying your breakfast. Only for you darling! *kissing emoji**

Before I had the chance to reply, my phone pinged again.

Khalil: *Don't get too full. We have an appointment with Jordyn today to look at some houses. Is three p.m. okay with you?*

I looked at the time on my phone. It was only nine a.m. I'd have plenty of time to sleep off this omelet.

Me: *Yes. Three is good. See you then. Thanks again for breakfast and the beautiful flowers. You made my day! *smiley-face emoji**

Before I could read his reply, my phone rang in my hand. It scared me. I completely forgot all about Malachi being on the phone.

"Hello!" I answered like I just didn't rudely leave Malachi hanging on the line while I texted Khalil. However, to my surprise it wasn't Malachi on the phone; it was the gate guard.

"Ms. Evans, this is the gate. I have a Malachi Richardson here to see you." *What the fuck?* This dude was really trying me. "Can I let him in, ma'am?" the guard asked.

I quickly reply to him, "No. Keep him at the gate please." With that, I hung up.

Thirty minutes away my ass. Now his ass wanted to be aggressive. Where was this energy last week? I text him to let him know we could meet up somewhere. I would never disrespect Khalil by bringing Malachi here.

Me: *I'll meet you at the Bicentennial Park by the lake. If you can find me, you can find it.*

Malachi: *If you're not there in twenty minutes… fuck this gate. I'll be at your front door, Passion.*

Me: *Oh, now you're full of "I want to see Passion energy." Stop tripping. I'll be there.*

Malachi: *Play me for a joke if you want to.*

"What-the-fuck-ever," I said to myself. I got up from the table, placed my empty plate in sink, and went upstairs to get my purse and shoes. I was already wearing a pair of navy, distressed jeans and a white, off-the-shoulder crop op. He didn't deserve makeup and fancy hair from me today, so I didn't make no extra efforts. With that thought, I picked up my phone again to read Khalil's reply.

Khalil: *Anything for you, baby. *kissing emoji**

At that, I smiled. I should actually thank Malachi. Looked like his presence and disappearance turned out better than I could've ever imagined. I was happy about where Khalil and I were headed now, and not even Malachi was gonna mess that up.

I jumped in my pink Range Rover and headed toward Bicentennial Park, which was about ten minutes from my house to go meet Malachi..

CHAPTER 12

As I entered the park, I could see a few cars sporadically parked, but there is only one that stuck out amongst all the luxury cars in attendance—a black Kia Optima. I called Malachi.

Ring! Ring!

"You're looking right at me, Passion. Come get in," he says with a smile in his tone

"What are you in?" I ignored his statement just to be difficult.

He exhaled loudly, letting me know he was frustrated with my antics, but I did not care one bit. "The black Kia. Come get in the passenger seat so we can talk."

Without replying, I hung up the phone, parked my car, and got out. I could feel his eyes on me as I approached his car, so I put a little twist in my hip. Suddenly, the driver's door opened.

"I got it. Don't get out, unless you want to walk around and talk," I said to Malachi as he stepped out of the car. He ignored me and continued around the car to open my door. Once I was seated inside, he walked back to his side and got in.

Looking me up and down, he said, "You look good."

I scoffed. "Thanks."

"Damn. Where's the sweet and giving woman I met in Miami?" he said with a smirk.

"You ain't funny," I said, rolling my eyes. "She's in Miami, where I left her."

"I said my bad, yo, for not reaching out and returning your calls. What you expect, Ajah!" *Oh, so he taking shots!?* I thought as he continued talking. "Anyway, can we start over? Let me fix my fuckup. I really did enjoy our time together."

"Nah... I can't. Things have changed now," was my response.

"In a week! What could've possibly changed?" he asked with a frown on his face.

"Look, what we shared in Miami was adventurous and fun, but here, back in the real world, you and I won't work," I said as nice as I could muster.

"Why? Because of dude?" he asked with slight anger in his tone. I didn't respond, just looked at him. "Yeah, that's what I figured. Talking about he's your best friend. Guess that nigga can't stand a little competition, huh! Well, I tell you what, I ain't 'bout the bullshit. I have too many options. Holla at me when you wise up," he said, dismissing me.

"Wow... like that, huh?" I chuckled.

"Straight like that," he replied.

"So why even bother coming to meet with me if you're going to have that attitude?" I asked, baiting him. How dare he think he can just diss and dismiss me? *Tuh!*

"Because I figured you'd be woman enough to let me make up my fuckup with you, Passion. I know I messed up, but business comes first, then everything else. I was hopeful you'd understand that and appreciate my efforts," he said, now facing forward like a child pouting.

He was right in a way though. I was being a bit difficult. His disappearance from my life didn't affect it much. It just slightly pissed me off. However, with me and Khalil trying this relationship thing, I didn't want to ruin what we could have with a one-night stand. So I had to be real with him and myself, period.

"I do appreciate your efforts, and I accept it for what it is. However, like I said, things have changed. My life is moving in a different direction. I really don't want animosity with you. I think you're an astonishing man."

He didn't say anything, just looked straight ahead. I could see his jaw clenching.

"Can we at least be friends? Keep in contact?" I asked. He looked over at me like I had two heads. I knew we'd been intimate, but I didn't feel it was that deep.

"Yeah. I'll get with you sometime," he said.

I just smiled. "Can I get a friendly hug?" I asked.

He chuckled. "Yeah."

I got out of the car, and he followed me around the back. Wrapped his arms around my waist, he ran his hands down to my ass and squeezed it. I just laughed 'cause he played too much.

"Let me take you to dinner while I'm here," he asked.

"When are you leaving?" I said, pulling back from his embrace to look up in his face.

"After you let me take you to dinner."

Shaking my head I just laughed. "Can I get back to you on that?" I replied. I didn't want to make any promises I couldn't keep.

"Sure. You better be glad I got business. Holla at me tho!" he said with a smirk.

"Okay. I will." And with that, we parted ways.

✳✳✳

The rest of my day was spent working from home, then later with Khalil, looking at houses, which I thought was crazy for several reasons, and I told him as much. After seeing three places that were not to our likings, we had dinner at the Cheesecake Factory. I had the most divine time with him, in this element. Relationship Khalil was magnificent and completely unique. Don't get me wrong, he was an amazing best friend—loving, caring, protective, and giving. However, boyfriend and relationship Khalil was attentive in a way that he listened and interacted with me on a level that made me feel like his universe revolved around me.

At the end of the night, we went back home, to the house we shared, and just simply talked about our day. I thought changing the dynamics of our relationship was going to be an extremely hard and weird transaction, but it was quite contrary. It was like this was what our friendship had been lacking all these years. I could see myself falling in love with Khalil, and that scared me as well as excited me at the same time.

We stayed up talking until around three in the morning, and then we both went to our respective sides of the house—and let me just say, the good-night kiss made me want to pull him to my side and in my bed. I'd never tasted lips so full and sweet. It was like there was candy growing from his mouth. It was enticingly delicious.

Khalil and I decided that we were going to date and take things slow, so I had to cool my jets—cold shower it is tonight. I woke up again to one of my favorite things in the morning, the smell of breakfast. A girl could get used to this. After completing my hygiene and taking a shower, I got dressed for a meeting I had with a gentleman who was opening up a new club in downtown Dallas and wanted me to plan his opening event. I expected to see ZaNita again when I got to the kitchen. However, I was greeted by a much better view—Khalil cooking in a tank T-shirt and gray sweatpants. Yeah… I could definitely get with this.

"Good morning!" I greeted him.

"Good morning, beautiful. How did you sleep?" He looked up from cleaning some fruit to greet me.

"Not very good, but I'll be alright." I fake pouted.

"Why didn't you call me over? I would have put you to sleep," he said with a smirk. I just laughed.

"Anyway...where is ZaNita?" Yeah let's definitely change this subject because the way he was looking, I wanted him for breakfast.

"Not here. This is all me, baby. I know how important breakfast is to you when you have time to sit down and eat it, so I cooked you some," he said with that sexy ass smile of his.

"Awww, thanks," I said, blowing him a kiss.

"I wanted to talk to you about something also," he said.

"Oh no… now, I know why you cooked," I replied, giving him a "what now" look.

"Calm down. I wanted to talk about us both getting tested. I know we are taking things slow, and I'm not trying to rush you into anything, but life does not always go according to plan. I don't want us to be unprepared or having any other delays in regard to our intimacy. When the time comes, I want to be able to have you anyway I want. Being that I am just out of a relationship and you…. well whatever, I want us both secure and comfortable when the time comes."

Look at my man, smart and sexy. "That's fine, Khalil. I completely agree. Set it up," I said.

We ate breakfast and both went about out day. Khalil had work, and so did I. After kissing each other see you later, Khalil helped me to my car and waited until I pulled off before he left behind me. *Such a gentleman my bookie is,* I thought as I drove away to meet my new client, Mr. Richardson, at his club.

CHAPTER 13

One month later...

Being in a relationship with Khalil had been wonderful. Dating him and taking our friendship to the next level was one of the best decisions I'd made in my life. I never did go to dinner with Malachi. However, I did plan his club opening in Dallas, and let's just say our encounter wasn't totally pointless, because I earned a hundred-thousand-dollar bonus for my services of planning his event. Guess I really did rock his world.

Khalil and I found a beautiful eight-bedroom, nine-and-a-half-bathroom house with a pool, media room, game room, and a guesthouse with three bedrooms and three and a half bathrooms, where Khalil had been currently living. He wanted it to feel like we have our independence from each other as our relationship grew. It's cute, weird, and fucking amazing to me.

Tonight we had plans to attend a Rihanna concert, and I was hyped 'cause that was my girl, and he knew that. I decided to keep my attire sexy chic because I wanted to be sexy and tease him a little. I dressed in a PrettyLittleThing fawn black, feather skirt bodycon dress with my Fetish peep-toed lace pumps from C. Louie. I was looking fly. I couldn't wait to see

Khalil's reaction.

As I was walking down the stairs to meet Khalil, I heard a ping from my phone. It's a text message from my bookie.

Khalil: *Ready to go my queen?*

I smiled. I loved it so much when he called me that.

Me: *Yes, sir. *wink emoji**

Khalil: *You know you ain't ready for that life!*

Me: *LOL! Don't underestimate me!*

I knew exactly what his freaky ass meant by that comment. Although we never discussed our sexual encounters with others when we had relationships in the past in detail to each other, I knew what Khalil was capable of. Since we started dating, we'd had a few conversations regarding our desires and fantasies. We both recently got tested and were disease free. I was ready to experience what I had all those years ago, plus some. All these late-night talks about it were not cutting it for me anymore. He was gonna beg for it tonight.

When Khalil walked in from the patio door into the living room, my whole cocky thought shifted. *Damn. I may be the one begging.*

He wore a pair of black True Religion jeans, matching black-and-red striped Henley shirt, showing all his muscular glory, and black Bally Hekem high-tops, and draped over his left arm was a black army bomber jacket. He looked comfortable, sexy, and delicious. *Fuck!*

Without saying a word, he walked over to me, pulled me into his arms by my hips, and covered my lips with his. His kiss was slow and full of passion. I felt it all over my body. I shivered from the electric currents flowing through my body from his kiss. Unable to hold back, I moaned onto his lips. He groaned in response.

Pulling my body closer, he moved one of his hands up to my cheek and the other behind my head, deepening the kiss. My hands begin to travel along his back, feeling his muscles with my fingertips. I squeezed him, trying to control my urge to get naked and make love to him right here in the living room. Removing his lips from mine, we made eye contact. It felt like I was looking at the stars. His eyes were shining so bright. We stared and smiled at each other.

"Hello, beautiful," he said.

It took a few seconds before I was able to catch my breath. Finally able to speak, I reply with a stammer, "H-Hello, handsome."

He chuckled. "Ready to go before we miss Rihanna, and you be sitting on my face all night instead?" he asked with this sexy grin on his face.

My eyes dropped instantly to his delicious lips. I cleared my throat. "Don't play," I said, trying to sound nonchalant. "I'll just do that when we get back later." I sassed as we both laughed.

I had been threatening Khalil with pussy, more like teasing him, for the past couple of weeks. He didn't know it though, but I was feenin' for him just as much as he was me. I just wanted to make sure I was totally ready to make that move because I knew once we crossed that hurdle, there was no going back, especially since I was already in love with him. Although we hadn't verbally expressed that love for each other in this new aspect we were in, I knew it was there because I felt it, which was way better than hearing it.

"Let me go upstairs and freshen up, and then we can leave," I said.

"Need some help?" he asked with an eyebrow raised.

"No. We'll definitely be late if you do that." I winked. I was already wet and horny, but I wanted to see Rihanna and wouldn't let my dickmatized desires stop that.

Khalil brought out his 2019 Bugatti Divo for our travels to the Verizon Stadium for the concert. I was in heaven. I loved fast cars. When we were teenagers, Khalil and I would build cars together and race them for money. It was an exciting time. Now he purchased faster cars for millions, and I couldn't be prouder of his new dynamic, but a part of me still missed being a grease junkie.

***

The concert was amazing! My girl Rihanna killed the stage, and her opening act Bornhustlaa let us all know he was here to kill the game. I was all for it. During the concert, I danced and jumped all over the place, while Khalil held my waist while grinding on me. He kept his face in my neck, kissing me during the slower tunes.

When Rihanna sang "Fool in Love", he sang it in my ear, sending shivers all down my spine. I hadn't stop smiling or dripping since. I couldn't wait to get home to show him how much I enjoyed having him as mine.

As we were leaving the theatre, I stopped in the restroom to freshen up. Imagine my surprise when I hear none other than Destiny right before I walk out of the stall.

"How could he be here with her. Best friend my ass," she said to whomever she was with.

"Destiny, why are you worried? You're here with that fine ass Malachi," said her friend.

Malachi? Naw, no way. That's the same Malachi from Miami.

"Because…" Destiny whined.

"Look, don't ruin this for me. I like Choppa. Just because Malachi made it clear he just want to fuck only, enjoy him why you can. My date actually lives in Texas, and we are clicking," her friend stated, putting her on blast.

"Girl, Choppa a dog just like Malachi, talking about y'all clicking." Destiny exhaled hard "I'm sorry, girl. I just thought that Khalil was it for me. He has it all, and I no longer have him. It hurts I gave him eight months of my life, Sabrina… that's a long time. Now he's all hugged up with Ajah fake ass. I hate her!" Destiny said with anger in her voice. I wanted to burst out laughing so bad.

"Stop whining, and fight for him. Get your man back. Fuck that bitch Ajah," said her friend, who I now knew as Sabrina.

"You're right! I'm not giving up on Khalil. He's mine, and Ajah gonna have to step down 'cause I'm coming back full force," Destiny replied, excited by the boost her friend had just gave her.

I was over this conversation and had heard enough. I stepped out of the stall. Destiny and Sabrina stood there with their mouths hanging open as I walked to the sink to wash my hands and touch up my lipstick. After checking myself over in the mirror, I turned to Destiny and said, "Game on, luv!" I walked out the restroom laughing.

When I approached Khalil, he asked me what happened, I told him nothing. I was just thinking about the rest of our evening and how I couldn't wait for dinner 'cause I was starving. He gave me a look as if he didn't believe me. However, he didn't call me on it. He just grabbed my hand, and we headed toward the exit.

CHAPTER 14

We went to a new restaurant near the venue called J'taime. It's reservation only, so it wasn't packed, which I liked. Khalil and I got a booth in the corner for privacy. Although he wasn't an athlete, he socialized and was photographed with a lot of celebrities, meaning sometimes he was mistaken for one, and it made it difficult to just chill most times when we were out.

"They have real good seafood macaroni here." Khalil informed me.

Before I could respond the waiter came over to take our drink orders. He did a little mild flirting with me, and Khalil was pissed. I thought him being territorial was sexy as hell.

"Don't get that soft ass waiter fucked up, Ajah," Khalil stated, looking serious.

"What?" I played bashful.

"Yeah... a'ight. Play with me. And why you sitting all the way over there? Come here. Let me feel some of that body heat," Khalil demanded. I just giggled. Yes, he has that effect on me. It was exhilarating.

As soon as I got closer, Khalil placed his right hand on my thigh and started a slow rub with his fingers on the inside of my thigh. I looked up at him from my menu, and he was staring at me, and then his eyes moved to mine. There was so much passion and lust in his eyes that my mouth started to water. I'd never seen this look from him before, and it had me ready to leave the restaurant right now. He leaned in, and his lips covered mine. I moved in even closer, and then his hand began to move further up my thigh with a squeeze. I moaned in his mouth.

"Ummm hmmm." Someone was clearing their throat.

Both of us pulled back slowly and turned our heads to see who had the nerve to interrupt us. To my surprise and displeasure, it was Malachi standing at the end on the right side of our booth.

"Well, isn't this a pretty picture?" he sarcastically said. "Hello, Passion! You look beautiful tonight."

Rolling my eyes I replied with my event-planner smile, "Thank you, Malachi. How have you been?"

Of course, he had to be messy. "Missing you," he replied with a mischievous smirk.

"Yo, bruh, move along with that bullshit. You're interrupting our private dinner," said Khalil with a clenched jaw.

"Fuck nigga—" Malachi started.

I cut him off. "No... no, we will not be doing this tonight." I started looking between the both of them. "Nice seeing you Malachi, but please move along. Good night," I said, trying to defuse the argument.

"Man... Passion, I will break yo' nigga neck!" Malachi threatened.

With that, Khalil started getting outta the booth.

"Khalil... No! Please!" I grabbed his arm, trying to bring his attention back to me "Malachi, please, you have no idea what you're up against. Please just go."

"Haha! You think I'm scared of doc? I'll shoot his head off before he gets to the end of his seat," Malachi said, reaching for his waist.

"Not if I get you first," I said, sitting my clutch on the table with my hand inside on my pink Beretta Pico. Malachi looked at me with a sly smirk.

"Fuck, I should've got to you first. He don't know what to do with all the woman you are."

"He knows exactly what to do with me, that's why I'm his. Please... just leave, Malachi," I said, mean mugging him.

"Okay, but I'll see you around, sweetie," Malachi said while looking at Khalil.

Khalil clenched his jaw. Malachi threw his hands up in a surrender and laughs while walking away. Khalil was fuming. His fists were tight, and he was pissed. I knew part of it was because I didn't let him get his hands-on Malachi, but he had too much to lose, and Malachi wasn't worth it.

After several minutes of silence, I figured I'd be the first to say something since this was all my fault. "Khalil?"

"Not now, Ajah," Khalil finally responded.

"Are you mad?" *Stupid question, Ajah,* I thought to myself.

His only response was to get up from the booth. "Let's just go. We'll order something on the way home."

Feeling defeated, I looked up at him. "He's not worth your freedom, Khalil. I was just trying to help."

Khalil didn't bother looking at me. "Yeah, I hear ya."

I hated that even though they didn't fight, or anyone got killed, Malachi still managed to ruin our night. "Please don't be mad. Don't let Malachi ruin our night," I pleaded.

Khalil didn't say anything else. He pulled out his wallet and left a $100 bill on the table and grabbed my hand to help me from the booth, and we headed to valet to get his car.

On the way home, we rode in silence. Khalil was brooding while I was strategizing. When we finally made it home, he pecked me on the cheek at the front door and headed to the guesthouse. Now I was horny and agitated. But I wasn't giving up without a fight. I was determined to get me some Khalil tonight.

After taking a much-needed, hot shower I walk into my bedroom to find Khalil sitting on the edge of my bed. He was wearing a black tank top and his baller shorts with black ankle sock and the Giuseppe slides I bought him for his birthday last year, looking handsome. I was in my blush-colored towel—go figure.

I walked over to the bed, hoping he didn't notice me ogling him, and began moisturizing my body, trying to be all nonchalant about his presence. He immediately took the coconut butter from my hands, applies a generous amount to his hand and started rubbing it into my right thigh.

"I'm sorry for how I ended our night," he said. I couldn't speak. His hands rubbing my body felt fucking amazing, and I was speechless. "I know you meant well. But you also know he would've been dead before I left that booth," he said as he continued to lotion me up.

"I was just trying to have your back," I said in a moan, closing my eyes. He gently pushed me to the bed and started rubbing cream onto my feet.

"By making yourself a target and putting my most precious gift in harm's way?" he said with heavy bass in his voice. My eyes popped open. "You mean the world to me, and I love you, Ajah. I got us. You need to learn to chill, okay?" He looked up, and we make eye contact.

"Okay," I replied in a voice I didn't recognize.

Leaning into me, slightly covering part of my upper half, Khalil rubbed his lips gently against mine, then kissed me. The kiss started off slow as one of his hands slowly moved up my side and the other hand moved up my thigh. Our tongues began intertwining. The kiss deepened. It was full of determination and passion. The hand on my thigh reached my bare pussy. I know he felt how wet I was.

He pulled away from the kiss and looked me in my eyes. "Tell me you want me as bad as I want you," he commanded.

"I want you," I replied in my sexiest voice with no hesitation. He growled.

Still looking me in the eyes, he separated my folds and rubbed his finger on the inside of my pussy, and then he placed one finger inside of me. I widened my legs and moaned. He leaned in and kissed my neck, moving that finger in and out, establishing a rhythm. My body began to rock with his finger, and then he added another and placed his thumb against my clit, applying pressure there.

"Ahhh," escaped my lips as I threw my head back.

Khalil removed his hand from my waist and untied my towel, making it drop behind me, exposing my naked body to him. "Fuck, Ajah," he said before he leaned down and placed my left nipple into his mouth, sucking and pulling on it, mixing delicious pain with pleasure. His fingers in me sped up. He moved his mouth to my right nipple, ran his tongue across it back and forward, and then he sucked it into his mouth and tugged on my nipple ring... hard. I exploded all over his fingers.

"Khalilllll!" I screamed.

"Yeah, baby. That's it. Give it to me... cum for me."

Taking the fingers he just had inside of me from my body, he then placed them in my mouth for me to taste myself.

"Mmmmm," I moaned.

He started moving lower, kissing my sternum stopping at the big puzzle piece tattoo that linked with his, and then he continued moving lower. When he got to my navel, he licked around it and tugged on my belly ring. He stopped right at my pelvis area and lifted up to take his shirt off. Still panting and trying to catch my breath from my orgasm, I sit up slightly and reach up to touch his smooth chocolate skin over his eight pack. He gave me a sly smirk.

"Like what you see?" he asked.

With that, I sat all the way up and kissed him on his stomach, then moved higher and licked around his nipple. He groaned. Pushing me back onto my back, he went back to kissing my stomach, then moved to my left thigh and sucked—surely leaving a mark. While moving toward my right side, he stopped and placed a kiss to my pussy, licking it up and down, then sucked on my clit. I thrust my pelvis toward his face. At that moment, he moved to my right thigh.

"Ughh..." I belted out.

He chuckled. "Don't worry, baby. I got you."

He sucked and bit my right thigh while his right hand rubbed and tugged on my breasts and nipples. I arched my back. The sensation from the bites and the rubbing had my head spinning. My back raised from the bed completely. I experienced the biggest orgasm I'd ever had with absolutely no penetration, and I thought I stopped breathing for a few seconds.

When I opened up my eyes again, Khalil was looking at me with concern in his eyes and a smile on his face.

"You okay, baby?" he asked.

"Y-Yeah. I'm good," I barely got out.

With that, Khalil stood from the bed and finished undressing, taking off his baller shorts. To my pleasant surprise, he has nothing else underneath. My mouth drops. Now I thought I remembered, but I was gladly mistaken. Khalil is much bigger than I recalled him being in college. There was no way we were beginning anything else until I had me a taste.

Looking him in his beautiful eyes, I got down on my knees and crawled over to the foot of the bed where he was standing. He licked his bottom lip. I bit mine. He walked over, closer to me, and I licked my lips.

"Can I have a taste?" I asked.

"It's yours, baby. You can have it however you want."

Getting off the bed I dropped to my knees in front of him. Looking up at him, I licked the tip and savored the precum that started to leak and moaned. *Fuck! His cum tastes sweet!* I placed the head in my mouth and twirled my tongue around it.

"Fuck, Ajah," he said with a grunt.

That's all the motivation that I needed. Laying my tongue flat, I put almost all of him in my mouth, tightened my jaws, and start sucking his long, perfect dick like my life depended on it. I wrapped my hand around what wouldn't fit in my throat and went to work.

"Ssssss." He hissed and threw his head back in ecstasy. "Yeah, baby... suck that dick like you love that shit."

I loved his dirty talk. It was making me wetter. His hand went into my natural curls, and I opened my eyes to look up at him. His handsome face showed how he was feeling. I sucked harder, applying more pressure and saliva using my mouth. Thrusting his hips faster, we began a musical rhythm with his cock and my mouth.

"Ajah... baby... fuck... I'm cumm—" Khalil shouted out, but I didn't need no warning—I was catching whatever he shot.

I went harder. I pulled him in my mouth deeper. He grunted. Abruptly, I tasted his sweet nectar as he unloaded in my mouth. I kept sucking until he grabbed the sides of my face and stopped me. He lifted me up by my underarms and started kissing me, pulling my body closer to his. He placed his hands on my ass and squeezed, then lifted me up. I wrapped my legs around his waist and felt him walking.

I thought we were going toward the bed, but my back got pushed against the wall instead. Next thing I knew I feel Khalil rubbing the head of his dick through my wetness, teasing my hole. Pulling out of the kiss, I reached between us and placed him exactly where I needed him to be and began inching down.

"Mmmmmm... sssssss." I hissed.

Now, I know I'm no virgin, but damn! Khalil had me feeling like one. I looked up into his eyes. He was staring right at me. He leaned in and kissed my lips gently at first, then picked up the aggression in his kiss as he pushed more inches into me.

"Ahhh… Khalil… baby," I growled into his mouth as he thrust up into me completely, and I broke our kiss, laying my head on his shoulder, trying to adjust to his size. He stilled for a moment.

"You okay?" he asked as he slowly twisted his hip and grinded in me.

Panting uncontrollably, I whimpered, "Yessss… ahhh… don't stop."

He began speeding up his thrusts, and I matched him, moving up and down with my hands on his shoulders.

Grunting, he called my name, "Ajah… shit, girl." He walked us over to the bed and laid me on my back, placed my legs into the crooks of his arms, and went to work on my pussy.

"Khalil… baby, y-y-you hitting my spot," I said, throwing my head back, arching my spine, and grabbing his biceps. He continued moving his hips and started going deeper. I exploded again. This time, squirting all over his abs.

"Fuck yeah," he grunted. "Give me one more, baby."

Reaching down, he starts rubbing my clit as he went deeper, moving my legs to my ears, taking advantage of my flexibility. *Thank you, yoga!* He did some kind of flex with hips and grinded harder in me again, and it's over. I came, screaming his name.

He pumped a few more times, and he was right behind me, grunting out, "Ajah," as he released his seeds into me.

Best fucking night of my life…

CHAPTER 15

His strong arms had my body encased in their warmth. The sun was shining through the curtains. I was in total bliss.

"Mmmm," I whimpered as I moved my body closer into his. I hated to move, but I have to use the bathroom. I slowly tried to move my body out of his embrace, while trying hard not to wake him.

"Where you going?" he asked with his deep, raspy early-morning vocals. *Drip, drip... There go my thoughts of leaving this bed. How could just his voice get me this turned on?* I wondered.

"Nowhere," I responded.

"Mmmm hmmm." He chuckled.

We were both still naked from the lovemaking sessions we had last night, too tired to move after our last few orgasms that we fell asleep intertwined. He began to move his hand up my body until he reached my left breast, massaging it sensually. He places a wet kiss on the back of my neck, and I twisted my neck so that our lips met—morning breath and all. It must be love. Our tongues rubbed against each other. I felt Khalil position his dick between my ass cheeks, touching my love vessel from the back, moving back and forth, spreading my wetness.

"Damn... all that for me, baby?" He teased.

"Please..." I begged.

"Please what?" he said into my neck.

"Give it to me... Khalil... please," I pleaded again, then pushed my ass into him and started rubbing against him. That got me the result I wanted, and he thrust into me fully. We both moaned.

"This what you want, baby?" he asked, licking my earlobe.

"Yessss…" I screamed out.

"This my pussy… you hear me, Ajah?" he said while squeezing my hip, going deeper inside of me.

"Yessss…. sir!" I said in a gasp.

"Tell me… I want to hear you say it," he demanded while pushing into me harder. We were still on our sided and my left leg was in the crook of his arm.

"Ahhh… Khalil… baby." He moved his hand from my waist to the front of me and gripped my clit between his thumb and forefinger.

"Say it…" He thrust again, hitting my spot.

"This your pussy… ahhh," I said in a groan.

"I can't hear you…" he grunted out as he placed me flat on my stomach, pushed up on his arms, and started pounding into me with vigor.

"It's yours… Khalil… It's yourssss…" I screamed out as I came so hard I blackout.

When I come to, I'm lying on my back, and Khalil was walking out of the bathroom, naked as the day he was born, with a washcloth in his hand. When he looked at me, he got this huge grin on his face.

"Welcome back, baby," he said as he walked over to me and placed the washcloth on my forehead.

"How long was I out?" I asked.

"Only a few minutes," he replied.

"What did you do to me?" I'm nervous because nothing like this had ever happened to me before.

He tilted his head. "I gave you this grade A dick!" I just looked at him. He laughed. "Come on. Let's shower. I'm starving and need breakfast," Khalil said over his shoulder as he walked back into the bathroom, back muscles, leg muscles and succulent ass on full display.

Damn, my man is fine ass fuck, I thought to myself as I gambolled out of bed with haste. I couldn't wait to get my hands all over his body again. Yeah, I was in big trouble. How I pass out from an orgasm and still look for more? I just shook my head at myself.

✳✳✳

"Let's go away together?" Khalil asked me as we were cleaning the dishes from breakfast.

"When?" I replied excitedly. I loved to travel.

"When are you available?" He turned to look at me, waiting for my answer.

"Me? You're the one with the demanding schedule. I'm my own boss. I can delegate," I said with my hand on my hip.

He chuckled. "Alright, boss lady. How about next weekend?"

Before I could answer, his phone started ringing. He looked at the screen, then laid it down, just for it to ring again.

"Dang, who blowing you up this morning, mister?" I asked with a frown on my face.

"Why?" he replied with a smirk.

"Why?" I said with a mug on my face. "Don't play with me, Khalil."

He shook his head and laughed. "Or what?" he asked as he walked over to me and grabbed two handfuls of my ass. His phone rings again. "Look," he said, showing me the phone "I don't know who it is. It says 'private'."

As soon as he shows it to me, it rings again. I snatch it from his hand and take off toward the living room. I heard him laughing in the kitchen.

"Hello, Khalil's phone." *Silence.* "Hellooooo!" **Click!** It rang again. "Ughhhh…"

Frustrated with the games, because I already had an idea who it is, I walked back into the kitchen, answered the phone, put it on the island, and placed it on speaker. I mouthed to Khalil say hello. He completely ignored me. He is not one for the bullshit games, period. Whomever it was hangs up.

"Why didn't you say anything?" I asked pouting.

"You know I don't play childish ass games. The people that benefits me are either stored in my phone or know not to block me," he replied as he pulled my face into his and gave me a deep, passionate kiss. I closed my eyes and wrapped my arms around his neck. His hands moved down my back, rubbing tenderly.

Mumbling against my lips, he said, "I love you, Ajah."

I pulled back to look him in his eyes and said, "You had me at hello!" We collectively burst out laughing.

Khalil pecked me on the lips again. "Come on, let's go shopping," he said as he pulled from my embrace, grabbed my hand, and led me to the stairs.

Once we were dressed, we headed out to the mall and spent the day shopping for our trip next weekend. On the drive to the mall, Khalil informed me that he had already planned where we were going to, and that was the Grand Palladium Jamaica Resort & Spa.

When he said let's go away together, he wasn't playing. Grand Palladium was luxury and romance all wrapped in one. My man was definitely a real one. I was thinking maybe New York somewhere. He went all out. I was all for it too. Anytime I could get some stamps on my passport was a great adventure for me! In all actuality, he could've said South Padre Island or New Orleans, and I would have been happy as long as we were together.

My love for Khalil had transformed, and I was falling more in love with him every minute of the day. He was right when he told me grown Khalil was nothing like college Khalil. His maturity reflected in the way he loved me and how he was fearless in his pursuit of our happiness together. I was overjoyed just thinking about what the future held for us.

After shopping for hours, I was beat and ready to get home and rest. Khalil said that we would be gone for a weekend, so I made sure to buy some revealing swimwear, as well as some sexy attire for dinner dates. I knew Khalil, and he loved trying new restaurants when he traveled, so I made sure that I purchased an outfit that'd have him thinking about having me for dessert while he ate dinner.

We finally made it home around eight in the evening. After stopping by the Cheesecake Factory to have dinner once we left the mall. Unfortunately, I fell asleep alone tonight because Khalil received a call around ten from one of his patients, who apparently got into a dispute with his wife and punched the wall so hard he broke his hand and forearm, which, according to Khalil, was probably the end of his baseball career. Although I admired Khalil's drive and dedication to his patients, I wanted to fall asleep in his arms tonight, so I couldn't care less about some idiot and his wife, but I knew this was something I had to get used to if I was going to continue this relationship. So I cuddled up with my pillow and hoped that tomorrow morning started like this morning did, just without the blackout.

CHAPTER 16

Jamaica

It was a splendid Thursday morning—yes, we started our weekend before Friday—at five a.m. when we boarded Khalil's private jet to Montego Bay, Jamaica. We spent the entire three-hour flight joining the mile-high club—it was fucking awesome!

When we reached Jamaica—the air, the atmosphere, everything—I was speechless! Sangster International Airport, where we landed, had the most astonishing view. I guess it didn't hurt that we were tourists that looked like money with this big ass plane Khalil had. Once we got to Grand Palladium, my mouth was in the sand. The suite that Khalil had for our stay was extravagant—four-poster, king-size bed, all-white plush sheets, balcony with a beautiful view of the beaches and the circular hotel pool, a stupendous bathroom with an orgasmic Jacuzzi tub, and two flat-screen televisions in the living room… I could live here.

It was only noon, and we had a chance to rest in between our mile-high explorations on the jet, so I was ready to get sexy and hit the beach. I put on my pink, sexy, strappy, high-leg, cutout, one-piece swimsuit with my Givenchy pink slides. I was looking fly, if I did say so myself.

When Khalil walked into the room, I started panting. He was wearing low-waisted, pink, tropical-print swim trunks, and his Givenchy slides matched mine—I made sure of it when we went shopping. He bit his bottom lip.

"Do a spin, baby. Let me look at you," he demanded, making the motion with his finger for me to turn around. As I did a three-hundred-sixty-degree turn, he whistled. "Damn, baby. You got that ass out too! Man… Ajah, you gotta cover my shit up," he said brusquely.

"Khalil… no!" I fake whined and pouted. Walking over to me with a smirk on his face, he placed his hands around my neck and gave it a slight squeeze.

"Ajah, don't fucking play with me. Cover my ass up, and let's go. That view is for me only," he said as he smacked my ass. **_Smack!_**

Fuck, I loved it when his dominant side manifested. It was the ultimate turn on. "Yes, sir," was my reply as I put on my white, sheer cover-up, grabbed my beach bag, and walked out the suite with Khalil hot on my tail.

✳✳✳

We were on the last day of our vacation, sitting on the balcony of the hotel restaurant, watching the sunset. This was one of the most extraordinary trips of my life. Khalil made sure that I did everything I wanted. We went jet-skiing, scuba diving, took a boat to a private island and made love in the sand, ate exotic, Jamaican cuisine, went skydiving, and shopped 'til we dropped. The conversation was flowing, and the wine had me buzzing. I was thinking of how much I loved this new dynamic we were in. Khalil was a remarkable man. Everything about him was perfect. The way he made love to my body had me sprung.

"I'll be right back, baby. This rum going right through me," Khalil said breaking me out of my daydream.

"Okay," I said, smiling wide as he kissed me before walking away.

After a while, the waitress came back and refilled my drink. It was then that I realized Khalil had been gone for about ten minutes. _I know it don't_ *take that long to use the bathroom. We could have gone to the room for him to air it out,* I thought with a laugh.

As soon as the idea left my mind, a waiter approached the table with a mini vanilla cake and a pink T-shirt with something written on the front in big white letters. The cake said *will*, and his shirt read *you complete me in every way*. He put the cake down and walked away. I was baffled, like what the heck was going on? That's so random. Then another waiter walked up. His mini cake said *you*, and his shirt read *my best friend & perfect lover*. He followed the other waiter. Now I was spellbound. *What was going on?* I began looking around for Khalil, but he was nowhere in sight. Next, a waitress walked up with a huge smile on her face. Her mini cake said *marry*, and her shirt read *you make my life brighter each day we're* together.

Instantaneously, tears started falling down my eyes, and my hands went to my mouth. "Oh my goodness!" I said out loud. She handed me a Kleenex and walked away.

As soon as she cleared my view, Khalil walked up with a cake in his hand, wearing a black Armani suit—looking delicious as fuck. His cake said *me* in huge letters with a question mark. Nothing was helping these tears now, so I just put the Kleenex down. When he was close enough to me, he dropped down to one knee beside my chair.

"Ajah, all my life I have loved you. You are my best friend and my perfect lover. I cannot imagine waking up every morning to anyone else but you for the rest of my life. I promise to love you, cherish you, honor you, and show you all the attention and affection I have in me. Ajah Natalie Evans, will you please make me the happiest man in the world and be my wife?"

Before he could finish completely, I was out of my seat. "Yesss! Yesss! Yesss!" I screamed, and I jumped on him, kissed my future husband all over his face, then on his full, sexy lips like we were the only ones in the restaurant.

Talking against my lips, he mumbled, "So I can move out the guesthouse now?" I laughed at his silly self. "I love you, Ajah," he said while softly kissing my lips, stealing my voice for a minute.

"I love you more, future husband." He pulled out the ring box and opened it. I gasped. A cushion-cut, halo, pink-diamond ring greeted me.

"Khalil! Oh my God! It's huge!" My eyes grew a couple inches just looking at it.

"This little ole thing?" he said with a smirk on his face. "It's only nine carats."

I looked up in his face and yelled, "Nine carats! Khalil! Wow!"

"Nothing is too much for you, baby," he replied.

I kissed him deeply as he picked me up by my ass, and I wrapped my legs around his waist. I couldn't wait to get back to our suite so I could show him just how much I wanted to be his wife, and then we could call our parents and Shavonne, if it wasn't too late. I was too ready to share my good news with my bestie and mommies. Of course, our parents were ecstatic. They all said the same thing.

"Finally. We've been waiting forever!"

I'm certain when we got off the phone, they were already planning our wedding. I tried to inform them before we hung up that I only wanted a small, intimate wedding with family, fifty or less people. However, I'm sure that went unheard.

Shavonne yelled so loud in my ear I hung up on her, then called her back. She wanted to fly out to Texas this week to plan, like I wasn't an event coordinator, or I was getting married tomorrow. We finished talking while Khalil prepared us a bath in the Jacuzzi tub. He was going all out with candles and rose petals. I was elated.

Khalil and I spent our bath time talking about when we'd get married. He wanted to be wed within three months, and I was all for it. He bathed me slow and sensually, making me clean and dirty at the same time. I rode him slowly as we stared into each other eyes. We christened our engagement.

After our bath, we made love all night until we passed out. Our flight home was for tomorrow at noon, so we could sleep in. Plus, my man owned the plane, so I ain't have no worries. I was going to really miss it here, but we'll always have Jamaica.

CHAPTER 17

On our way home from the executive airport, we stopped at the gas station to fill up. I had a few errands to run for a corporate convention I was planning in two days, and Khalil wanted to make sure that the car was on full when I got behind the wheel.

"You want anything from out of the store?" he asked.

"Naw I'm good."

Before closing the door, he replied, "A'ight."

Watching him walk toward the store, I murmured, "Damn, my man's walk is something serious."

As soon as Khalil cleared the doors to the store, someone was knocking at my window. Taking my eyes off the doors, I looked to the side to see who it was. I instantly dropped my head and heavily exhaled when I saw Malachi standing there.

"You've got to be fucking kidding me," I mumbled to myself, shaking my head.

I didn't bother letting the window down. I just looked back at him like he was insane. Before he could get a word out of his mouth to me, I watched Khalil walking up to the car from my peripheral. *Fuck!*

"If it ain't the good doc." Malachi laughed, backing away from my window.

I tried opening my door, but Khalil pushed it closed before I could get it all the way opened. Before Malachi could utter another word, Khalil raised his hand and knocked him out—no words, just force behind his punch.

Malachi hit the ground hard and stilled. I gasped.

Some guy was coming up behind Khalil. "Baby...behind you!" I screamed at the window.

Abruptly, Khalil pulled his gun from his waist and pointed it at the guy behind him on his left. "Give me a reason, please!" Khalil barked. "Y'all niggas stupid as fuck. Tell yo' boy when he finally wakes up if he don't stay away from my girl, he won't be getting up next time." With that, Khalil walked backward to the driver's side, pumped the gas, then got into the car.

During this time, Malachi never got up, and his friend just stood there mean mugging me as I eyed him, watching my man's back with my hand on my gun in my lap. As we drove off, I wait for the argument, but it never comes.

"Baby, you good?" I asked.

Silence.

"Khalil, you can't be mad at me. I didn't do anything."

He just looked at me.

"Ughhh... whatever." I pouted, folding my hands over my chest.

When we came up to a red light, he reached over the console, grabbed my face, and kissed me, then winks at me as he pulled back. I just shake my head and chuckle.

"I love you, clown," I said to him.

"I love you more, big head," he replied.

By the time we make it home, I want a nap, but duty calls.

"Baby, I'll see you in a few hours," I told Khalil as I walked toward the front door.

"I'll be gone for a few hours too. I just got called in to help one of my patients, so I'll be in later," he responded, following me to the door. Suddenly, I'm squeezed between Khalil and the door. "Be good while I'm gone," he whispered in my ear.

"Yes, sir," I purred.

"I'll text you when I'm on my way home. Be naked." He instructed while licking my ear. The gesture makes me shiver.

"Mmmm... Yes, sir," I moaned.

"Good girl." He kissed me on my neck and opened the door for me. Then we went our separate ways.

After being gone for several hours, I made it home just in time to let the movers in. I was having them move all of Khalil's things from the guesthouse to the main house—my little surprise to my fiancé. Because there was no way I was sleeping without him ever again, unless one of us was out of town on business. In the meantime, I went to the kitchen to start dinner... seafood mac and cheese, T-bone steaks, and asparagus—his favorites.

I wanted our first day back to be exceptional. There was so much to do before Khalil got back. I needed to get dinner finished, make sure his things were organized after the movers leave, shower, and be ready to be waiting naked at the door.

Ring! Ring!

I get pulled out of my thoughts of tonight's plans by my ringing phone.

"Hello, trick," I said, to Shavonne,

"Hello, Mrs. Black!" She joked.

"Ahh… Girl! I know! Who would have thought that I would be Khalil's wife?" I yelled into the phone, ecstatic.

"Girl… please! I knew when you threatened to move out his house, and he bought a four-million-dollar house, so you'd continue to stay with him and not get your own place. Then he stayed in the guesthouse of the home *he bought* just so he could pursue you to your heart's desire. That man was destined to be your husband, sis!" My friend always knew how to make shit sound extraordinary.

"Whatever!" I said before we both laughed because we knew she was telling the truth. "What you got going on? I miss you," I asked her.

"I know our little weeklong playtime together was over too fast, especially when big head crushed our party." I laughed at her goofy self

"Not too much on my baby, now."

"Mmm… now he yo' baby?" she said, getting sassy.

"Did you not get the picture I sent you of my engagement ring? That's bae!" I said, rolling my neck like she could actually see me.

"Yeah, I feel that." Shavonne chuckled.

"Hold on one second. Let me get rid of these movers." I walked over to the patio door, signed the necessary paperwork, and tipped the movers. I am beatific about this surprise. "Hello? My bad. You still there, Shavonne?"

"Yeah, I'm here. You couldn't just take the phone with you, slow girl?" She laughed.

"It's charging. If I would've moved it, you would've heard the dial tone, punk," I told her big-head self.

Conceding, she replied, "I feel ya! So what's up with our wedding. Give me a date and my duties as maid of honor so I can be ready."

"So it's going to be in October. Khalil gave me a three-month deadline. I want to keep it simple. There's this villa in Grand Prairie, not far from where we live, that I'm thinking about booking. Once that is done, I'll have more information," I said, letting her in on my plans.

With a laugh, she replied, "Three months? That's more time than I assumed he would give."

"Girl, me too!" I laughed.

"You too what?" Khalil said, scaring me. I did not hear the door alarm beep when he came in. Good thing he just missed the movers. He came further into the kitchen, walked up behind me, then started kissing on the side of my neck right below my ear, and then came around and kissed me slow on the lips.

"Shavonne said she's surprised that you gave me three months to marry you," I said, breathless.

"Shit, if it were up to me, we would've come back from Jamaica as husband and wife," he replied with a smirk.

"Awwwww…" Shavonne chimed in my ear. I almost forgot she was on the line. I put her on speaker, and then I turned back to the counter to finish up prepping dinner.

"I want a Khalil," she said, not knowing she was on speaker.

"Well, this one is taken," Khalil said. "What's up, Vonne? How's Miami?"

"Hey, bro! It's okay. The hustle still strong. I'm just missing my baby mama."

He laughed. "Well, you need to move to Texas 'cause she ain't going nowhere unless we're touring the country together," he said with finality.

She just sucked her teeth. "Whatever, big head."

"I'ma go shower. Want to join me?" he whispered in my ear while licking my lobe.

"Khalil… baby, stop," I whimpered, trying not to moan. "I have to finish up here," I whispered back.

"Y'all really suck at whispering. Call me later, if you can, boo. Love you both," Shavonne said.

"Love you too!" we said in unison.

"Alright, baby. I'ma go over here to shower. I'll be back for dinner," he said.

"Over where, Khalil?" I smirked.

He tilted his head. "To the guesthouse, Ajah! You alright?"

"Yes, baby. I'm good," I said to him, smiling to myself.

With that he walked out the patio, toward the guesthouse. I wanted him to be surprised when he saw that I moved all his stuff, so I didn't warn him beforehand. Several minutes later, I heard the back door open. I looked over my shoulder to see Khalil walk into the house with a huge smile on his face. I giggled.

"Ajah, my love, where is all my stuff?" I could hear the smile in his voice.

"Upstairs in our room," I said, blushing at him.

He smirked. "So now it's our room?"

I held up my ring finger, showing him my engagement ring. "Until we move, if ever, it's ours, baby," I said all sassy with my hands on my hips.

He walked over to me and grabbed the back of my neck, then began softly rubbing his lips against mine. My eyes automatically closed. He licked my bottom lip, then bit it, pulling it into his mouth. He started moving his hands down my back and grabbed my ass.

"For life," he mumbled against my lips.

I could only nod my head. I was in a state of euphoria. He lifted me up by my ass and placed me on the island. Moving his lips down to my neck, he stopped. I opened my eyes and stared at him.

"Don't move," he commanded.

"What?" He pecked me on my lips, then walked toward the living room area.

I couldn't believe he just left me hanging like this. Suddenly, I hear Fatty Koo "Chills" begin to play throughout the house. I smiled and shook my head. Khalil walked back into the kitchen, jacket and shirts gone.

"Thank you, Jesus," I whispered. My man's body was absolutely beautiful muscles bulging, tattoos on full display, abs on swole. He was a walking sex symbol and all mine.

The sunlight smiles,
Faithful every day for you.
No one can come close to the,
Joy you bring to me.

The song boomed through the surround sound. *Damn, I love this song. It makes me feel so sexy,* I thought to myself. I maneuver my body closer to the edge of the island and spread my legs wider. I want him to have all the room he needs.

He maneuvered his body between my legs and clutched his left hand into my hair, tight, making a fist, then tilted my head back so he could get to my neck. His right hand was moving up my left thigh, getting closer to my shorts that I am bare beneath. There's nothing stopping his pursuit to my pussy but my shorts, which he'd already made his way into. When he sucked harder on my neck, my moan came out like a sob. He touched my pussy. My breathing accelerated, and I'm panting 'cause he got me in heat. He pushed through my folds, putting his finger inside of me.

"Ahhhh… Khalil," I said as I clasped my walls around his finger and start grinding on it. I wanted to feel him inside of me so bad, right now. His finger was not enough.

Before I could open my mouth to beg, he said, "Damn, girl, you so wet… all that for me, baby? You ready for this dick, Ajah?"

"Yes… please," was my mumbled response.

"Please what, baby?" He loved to make me beg.

"Khalil…" I pleaded.

He removed the finger from inside me, because he knew what I wanted, then placed the finger—soaked from my juices—in his mouth.

"Mmm… The sweetest shit in the world, that's what my pussy is," he said, looking me deep in my soul through my eyes. He removed his hand from my hair and placed his hands at his waist, unlatching his belt.

"Khalil…" I whined. Just the thought of having him inside of me was driving me wild.

"Yes, baby?" he responded, now looking back up at me.

"I need you," I said, humping the air 'cause now I feel completely empty without none of him touching me.

I moved closer to him and rubbed my hands on his chest. It jumped, and I pinched his nipples between my fingers, then twisted a little just to give him some pain I know how much that turned him on. He grunted. I climbed down from the island and dropped to my knees in front of him. I looked up at him, waiting for our eyes to connect. When they did, I removed his hands from his belt and finished the task myself. His zipper was next. I placed my face into his now-open pants and sniffed. His manly musk was intoxicating, and I could feel my juices flowing down my thigh.

I gripped the waist of his exposed briefs and pulled them down along with his pants. His cock sprung free. It was chocolate, long, thick, smooth, and without blemish, with a mushroom head. My mouth watered at the memory of the taste of him. I put the head in my mouth and twirled my tongue around it, then placed as much of him as I could into my mouth. The rest was in my hand, and I began to massage his shaft to match the rhythm of my mouth. He tasted so good, like rich Godiva chocolate. I could suck his dick forever.

"Sssssss... mmmm."

His head fell back, and his hips began to move. I closed my eyes, savoring the precum dripping from his tip, and a beautiful rhythm manifested as I pleased him with my mouth. What felt like immediately, Khalil stopped his movements. I opened my eyes to see him looking down at me.

"Get up, Ajah," he groaned.

With my tongue still flat and my mouth still wrapped around his cock, I slowly pumped him a few more times, then dragged him from my mouth with a pop. He helped me to my feet and lifted me by my arms back onto the island. I welcomed him back home, between my legs. My eyes are on his manhood. It's so fucking marvelous that my mouth is dripping again. Khalil placed himself at my opening and breached me with the first inch, moving his hips back and forth, slowly teasing my body. He clutched my hair into his fist, pulled my face up to his, and kissed me as he thrust into me all at once. I wanted to throw my head back, but his grip on my hair didn't let up.

"Ahhhhh!" I scream. My back curves, and I grab onto his triceps. "Fuck... Khalil... Yess."

He pulled me closer to him, going deeper and harder. Now his hands were no longer in my hair. They were both around my waist, and his mouth was on my nipple ring, tugging it between his teeth. My hands moved to his head. I pulled him closer to my chest. His tempo was driving me insane. Fatty Koo is in the background singing about chills up her spine. I feel like I'm in a whirlwind.

"Stay with me, Ajah," I heard Khalil say.

I definitely don't want to black out again. He's thrusting and twisting his hips, hitting my G-spot to perfection repeatedly. I couldn't do anything but meet his plunges. He felt so fucking good, and I told him so. He grunted, still assaulting my breast with his tugs. He draws back and meet my eyes.

"Cum for me, baby… let me feel you."

My walls clasp around his shaft. I loved when he talked that talk during sex. His right hand moved from my waist to my clitoris. He placed the exact amount of pressure to my nub I needed to get me there, and I exploded all over him with a scream. Khalil pulled out of me, took a step back, and placed me on my feet. My legs were weak, so he balanced me in his arms, taking all my weight. He was so fucking strong.

He turned me around, bent me over, and with his fist back in my hair, put my face on the island. While behind me, he centered his dick to my pussy and thrust right into me. We both let out a groan. He started off slow, giving me a brief second to adjust to his size. Before long, his thrusts picked up, and we were following the rhythm that was surrounding us with the music.

Finally feeling like I was breathing on my own, now was time to boss up. I began winding my hips and twerking on his dick. He released his grip from my hair and grabbed my hips and grinded into me.

"Yeah, throw that pussy back."

Smack! Smack!

"Nah, don't slow down… Throw that pussy to me," Khalil told me.

He reached his hand around me and played with my breast. I could feel his chest on my back and his face on my neck. I turned my head, and he kissed me. His tongue was in my mouth, slow and sensual, while his hips played a lethal game with my body. I felt that all too familiar tightness in my belly. I grinded harder. He lifted his body from mine. Standing up, he bended at his knees, going deeper. In and out. In and out. Twisting his hips like magic.

"Right there… baby… don't… ahhh… stop!" I screamed out in a moan.

"Right there," he groaned. "Cum with me, Ajah. I'm close."

"I'm cumming… don't stop… ahhhh! Khalillllll!"

I'm gone. And he followed me over, releasing his seed into my womb. My knees gave out, and my arms went limp. He caught me in his arms. We slid down to the floor, with me on top of him—chest to back. All that can be heard was our labored breathing and Fatty Koo still going strong. I chuckled.

"What's so funny?" Khalil asked.

"Good thing all the food is already in the oven. We would've starved 'cause I ain't no good after that." He chuckled.

"You know I got you, greedy, but how you thinking about food after I just laid it down?"

"Because now that you've worked me, I'm hungry," I told him.

We both laughed, followed by a comfortable silence that fell over us.

"I love you, Khalil," I said as I turned my head to the side to look at him.

"Yeah. Good dick. It'll do that to you," he said with a chuckle.

I pushed up and looked back at him. There's that sexy smirk of his again.

"Whatever, clown," I said, then hit his bare chest.

"Come shower with me in *our* bathroom," he told me, no longer asking.

"Okay, let me turn the food down."

We headed to the shower. I washed his body, and he washed mine... seductively, which led to me sitting on the bench in the shower while he squatted down and ate my pussy like a starved man until I squirted my juices all over his face, then screamed for mercy.

After our shower, we ate dinner by candlelight outside on the patio as India Arie *Voyage to India* album played on repeat. He told me about how he spent the day treating a tennis player that dislocated her adductor muscles using a sex swing she got from her husband for their anniversary. It was hilarious.

After cleaning the kitchen together, we headed upstairs to bed. I fell asleep that night in what has become my favorite place to be in the world—wrapped in Khalil's embrace and listening to my lullaby—his heartbeat—as I fell into a deep sleep.

.

CHAPTER 18

Khalil and I had been engaged for three weeks now. I was ecstatic about becoming Mrs. Khalil Jerome Black. The villa I wanted to rent for our wedding in Grand Prairie was available. However, I discovered the venue the company had in Arlington was much bigger and available, so we went with that one instead. Khalil was way more involved than I thought he would be, and I was impressed that he wanted to be a part of the process. It showed me that he was in this for real. He went from venue to wedding store with me, went to menu tastings without argument, and helped me battle our parents about who to invite. It was magnificent to have his support.

We both decided that we'd have one witness stand with each one of us during the ceremony. Our colors were coral and baby blue. Shavonne and our mothers were flying down in two weeks so we could go wedding dress shopping. It was going to be an event. I knew that for sure. I was super nervous about how the three of them together were going to be overwhelming and so much fun.

Khalil insisted on placing a wedding announcement in the local newspaper, in print and online, which ended up turning into a huge mistake because not only did all his patients and staff think it meant they all could attend our nuptials, but the private phone calls had escalated times ten over. It became so obnoxious that Khalil wanted to change a number he had for ten years. He couldn't just immediately change his number because of his business. Nevertheless, I could see it about to happen. He had already purchased another phone line and was in the process of getting everyone familiar with that new number.

It was crazy that such drastic measures had to be taken because this chick Destiny didn't know how to let go. If I could just get my hands on her for ten goods minutes, I was sure I could convince her to stop all this messy shit she was doing. I felt her though. Having Khalil as a mate would put your wildest dreams to shame because there's no way to dream up the dynamics of what he was made of. Waking up and going to sleep with him in and near me was a must have I wouldn't trade for the world. I'd also like to think that he was just that way with me, but if she experienced 10% of what I got on the daily, her plight to have more was understandable as well as annoying as hell.

✳✳✳

We were laid in bed wrapped in each other's embrace—my back to his chest and his face in my neck like he needed to breathe my scent to rest. Khalil's phone had been ringing for the past few minutes nonstop, and he hadn't even flinched from the noise. That's how exhausted he was tonight. He'd missed four calls already. The first one was what woke me up from my sleep.

I was fuming because I knew he was tired from his trip to California he'd just came in from a few hours ago. I told him to put his phone on silent before he came to bed at one o'clock this morning, but the hustler in him wouldn't let a moment of silencing his phone happen, which is why I couldn't understand how he was sleeping through his ringing phone.

I shook him slightly. "Khalil... baby, please answer your phone."

"Get it for me," he murmured into my neck, where his face was buried.

"It's over by you. Just answer it or silence it. That's the fourth time it's rang. I can't fall asleep with the noise," I said with an attitude.

"Ughhh!" His arms left me "You waking me up for this bullshit ass phone. It better be some money." The way he grabbed the phone, I thought he was going to toss it across the room. Instead he tossed it to me, almost hitting my thigh, got up out of the bed, and walked toward the bathroom.

"Rude!" I said as I rolled over to face him.

"I'm sorry, baby," he said over his shoulder.

At that moment, the phone stopped ringing. I sat up and leaned my back against the headboard slightly and grabbed his phone off the bed to place it on silent. It immediately started ringing again.

"Hello?" I answered with attitude. There was silence on the other end, but I could hear some heavy breathing. "Look, we are tired of you and this bullshit. We are trying to rest. Why won't you just move on and leave us alone, Destiny?" I called her out.

"I need him. Please let me talk to him," Destiny said, proving what I already knew.

"At three o'clock in the morning? For real chick? Are you serious?"

"Pleaseeeee," she said, sounding drunk.

I exhaled. Just as I went to hang up on her, Khalil resurfaced back into the bedroom from the attached bathroom and got back into bed, then wrapped his arms tight around my waist, and laid his head on my stomach like his phone wasn't in my hand. I put the phone on speaker and dropped it on the bed near his face.

"Baby, she says she needs you."

"Who is she? A patient?" he asked while kissing on my exposed belly.

"No. It's me, Khalil," Destiny said loudly, not realizing she was on speaker.

"Destiny?" he asked with a frown on his face.

"Yes! We need to talk," she said.

He sucked his teeth. "So talk," he said as he raised his body on his elbows and started kissing up my sides.

"In person," she demanded.

"Look, I don't have time for the bullshit, Destiny. What you want?"

She gasped. "I can't believe you're acting like this, Khalil! Like I never meant anything to you."

I was two seconds from cursing her out. Khalil began moving his kisses downward toward my pelvis and bit me. I flinched. I knew he was trying to distract me, but I didn't care. I was furious, but I loved his mouth on me, so I just looked down at him and remained quiet.

"Spit it out, Destiny," he murmured into my hip.

"I'm pregnant." She burst out all confident.

He lifted his head from my skin. "Congratulations," he said, looking up at me with a smirk, but I was not laughing. I was pissed at this whole, dumb three-in-the-morning conversation with his ex.

"It's yours," she said with a smile on her face. You could hear it through the phone.

He chuckled. "Impossible," he said decisively.

"What?" she said now with uncertainty in her voice.

"I had a vasectomy five years ago." He winked at me. I shook my head and giggled with my hand over my mouth. He was lying, and I knew it.

"No you did not, Khalil! Stop lying!" Destiny whined.

His lips went back to my body. He started nibbling at my lower abdomen, just a few inches shy of my pussy. I flinched again and placed my hand on his head and rubbed his hair.

He pulled back and said, "I did. You knew I didn't want kids. My job is too demanding, but congrats, and good luck to you with your new addition," he said, picking the phone up to end the call.

Something must've let her know he was done talking. She yelled out his name with urgency, "Khalil!"

He didn't respond just threw the phone down and licked my mons. I widened my legs and lifted my ass a little to try and maneuver him lower where I was leaking and waiting for him.

I thought she hung up 'cause there was complete silence, and then she said, "Okay, I'm not pregnant, but look… I miss you, and I know Ajah is just your rebound to make me mad. Stop playing these games with her, and come home, Khalil. I forgive you for how you've been acting."

When she said that, his nose went between my folds, and he began to lick my pussy and suck on my clit. I couldn't speak. I moaned.

"Khalil? Khalil… you still there?" Destiny asked.

He licked on my clit, then sucked on it harder. I moaned louder. There was no holding back when Khalil put in work on my body. I could tell she heard me.

She yelled his name again, with anger this time, "Khalil!"

His hands went to my breasts, and he squeezed my nipple while his face remained buried between my legs. I arched my back and started moving up and down with his tongue. I was so close. With his tongue, Khalil continued to lick my pussy. He moved one of his hands from my breast and placed his fingers in me.

Lifting his mouth briefly, he said in between licks, "Are… you… gonna… cum… for… me… baby?"

"Ahhh… Yessss… s-sir," I whimpered.

"Fucking really, Khalil!" Destiny yelled out.

Khalil pinched my nipple harder. "Cum, Ajah… She wants to hear you, baby," he said, not bothering to whisper.

"I hate you and that bitch!" Her yells echoed through the room.

Khalil sucked on my clitoris again while rolling my nipple between his fingers. My entire upper body came from the bed as my body shook, and I exploded into his mouth.

"Ahhhh… shitttttt, Khalil!" I yelled out.

"Mmmm. Sweetest shit in the world. That is my pussy," Khalil said. He kissed my pussy lips twice, then lifted up his head and smiled at me. "I love you, Ajah Black."

"I love you more, Khalil Black," I said out of breath with a giggle.

I was still panting, trying to catch my breath when Khalil started kissing up my stomach, then between my breasts, where he stopped to lick around my now-sensitive nipples. I placed my hands on his shoulders and rubbed down his back. He moved higher and kissed my neck. He positioned himself directly between my widened legs and kissed my lips. I could taste myself on him, turning me on more.

I sucked on his tongue so I could savor my taste. He moved his hips as we kissed and stroked his cock up and down my folds. I hefted my hips, telling his body to penetrate mine. Khalil moved his left hand between us and slowly teased my clit with the head of his dick, rubbing it up and down repeatedly. I opened my eyes. He was looking right at me, observing my love faces.

As we stared deep into each other's eyes, he slowly moved himself into my body, inch by slow inch. It was the most spectacular and frustrating experience, but as bad as I wanted him to stop teasing me, I was savoring the delicious tease he was giving me. I was dripping wet. I could feel it going between my ass cheeks. He pulled out all the way, bit his bottom lip, then propelled into me.

"Ahhhh! Khalil… baby… shit!" all came out my mouth at the same time. I was feeling all kind of pleasure pain.

"Yes, baby… That's it. Take all this dick." He placed my right leg on his shoulder, putting himself deeper and deeper with each stroke. "That's right. Throw that pussy back… mmmm… Shit, girl. I love this wet… tight… pussy," Khalil said with a groan.

"Yess-ss… ssss!" He had me speechless. I could already feel my orgasm building in the bottom of my belly.

"Ajah, cum for me baby… Cum all over your dick, baby."

Speeding up his pace, I sped up right along with him. I was chasing that nut, pushing me right to the edge.

"I'm cumming! Don't stop! I—Ahhhhhhh!"

"I ain't never stopping, baby. This pussy too good."

As soon as he said that, my body started convulsing. I was shaking from my head to my toenails, completely finished, or so I thought. Khalil removed my leg from his shoulder and started grinding into me slow and strong, rotating and rolling his hips while burying his face in my neck, sucking and kissing right below my ear.

"I love you, Ajah… nobody but you, baby," he mumbled into my skin.

After he grinded in me for a few more minutes, I finally gained the feeling back in my fingers, and I began rubbing his back. I bent my knees up toward the headboard and widened my once-still legs a little more, displaying my flexibility. I rotated my hips, matching his rhythm. He groaned.

"Baby, you feel so fucking good." I panted as I squeezed my pussy muscles.

"Ahhhh… shit," he moaned.

I started going harder. He picked up his pace and grunted, pushing up on his arms like he was doing a push up, looked down at me directly in my eyes. He was so deep. I swear he was coming out my throat. Sweat was dripping from his body onto mine, and it was ecstasy. After going hard for a few more delicious minutes, we climaxed together—me with a scream, and him with a loud groan that was sexy as hell.

Khalil's arms came down, and his upper body was resting on mine. I closed my eyes and breathed him in, locked my arms around his neck, and wrapped my legs around his waist. He was fully on top of me now but still not close enough for me.

"Let's elope," I said into his neck.

His head popped up, and he looked me in the eye., "All I had to do was make you cum three times in a row to get you eager to marry me?" he said with that sexy smirk and licked his lips.

"No. The orgasms are bonus! You defending me, loving me unconditionally, protecting me, being attentive to my wants and needs, and being the best man, any woman could want or need... plussss this huge ass diamond." I laughed. "I want to be your wife more than anything because you are *you*, not for the reason that you just sexed me into a new day."

He leaned down and kissed me. The kiss was filled with so much love and passion. I could feel him growing inside of me once again. I moaned at the thought that my love for him turned him on. We begin moving. My legs still around his waist and his face back buried between my shoulder and neck.

"Tell me when and where, baby. Whatever you want... you got" he said before he kissed my shoulder.

He flipped us over our bodies, still attached. I was now on top. I started slow winding my hips, adjusting my body to his girth. He grabbed me around my waist and began thrusting upward. I placed my hands on his chest and twerked on my dick until I climaxed two more times. When he finally released his seeds inside me again, I was in a sweet, blissful state.

As we lay side by side, with heaving chests, I thought to myself, *I know tomorrow morning is going to be a late one my man had worked me over something proper like.* We both fell asleep in that exact position—together, exhausted, my head on his chest, and his hand on my ass. Pure bliss.

CHAPTER 19

'Til Death Do Us Part

One week later, we were in our backyard with our parents, Shavonne, and Khalil's best friend, Lawrence, getting married. I was an only child, so I didn't have any siblings to stand by my side. Khalil's brother, Kairo, was sadly killed when he was sixteen by a drunk driver, and his sister Kaari was extremely upset that her job planned a trip for her that couldn't be cancelled. If no one else was here, we definitely wanted our families here with us, so Shavonne setup some kind of tech geek link that allowed Kaari to watch us from her laptop.

I wore an ivory-colored, tea-length, spaghetti-strapped sheath dress with a lace top with my Dolce and Gabbana lace booties Khalil bought me last year for my birthday. Khalil wore a cream-colored Armani suit with a soft-pink button up shirt with the top two buttons undone. We were sexy, chic, and formal.

It was August in Texas—hot and dry. We rented a tent with air conditioning for comfort during the ceremony.

Our mothers cried as my father walked me down the aisle. Khalil had tears in his eyes as he pledged his undying love for me. I sobbed like a baby as I told him how much I was grateful that he chose me for his wife and how I loved him to the moon and back. When the pastor announced us as husband and wife, Khalil kissed me like we were alone, and to me, the room did disappear. The only sound I heard was our hearts beating as one. By the time we finally came up for air, we actually was alone.

"Mrs. Khalil Jerome Black… damn, that sounds sexy. I think I'll get it tattooed on my pussy. What you think, husband?" I said as I looked up into my husband's eyes. He just chuckled and shook his head. "What?" I asked with a frown.

"You are perfect. That's what," he responded and kissed me again.

"Will y'all come on so we can eat? Dang!" Shavonne yelled from the patio door.

Khalil grabbed my left hand, entwined our fingers, and kissed my ring. I blushed and buried my face in his side as we walked into the house to join our family. *I am the luckiest woman in the world.*

CHAPTER 20

"How long we have to wait for babies?" Khalil's mom, Evelyn, started as soon as we walked into the house.

"I'm ready when she is, Ma," Khalil replied with a smirk on his handsome face.

I looked up at him. "Dang, baby. Way to have my back," I said with a laugh.

He grabbed my face and kissed me before pulling me toward the table, where everyone was already seated.

ZaNita's catering company prepared the intimate dinner for us. It included favorites of both Khalil's and mine—homemade mashed potatoes, T-bone steaks, chicken masala, broccoli with cheese sauce, corn on the cob, baked potatoes, spinach rice, fresh string beans, stuffed garlic knots, Hawaiian rolls, and a beautiful three-tier vanilla-bean-and-strawberry wedding cake made and delivered—via Khalil's private jet—from Kaplan's Kakes in Hollywood, FL—my favorite bakery. I was in phat girl heaven.

"You guys have plenty of time. Don't pressure them, Evelyn. They haven't even been married a month yet. They are two young kids with demanding careers. Let them settle, and then we'll annoy them with baby talk," said my mom, Annette, surprising me immensely.

Khalil and I looked at each other, then burst out laughing. "Ma… really! Because weren't you just telling me how much you're ready for a baby the day I came back from Jamaica?" I said.

"Stop bringing up old stuff before you get in trouble, young lady. You are not too old for a good spanking," my mother stated with a stern face.

With that, everyone started laughing, including my mother. The rest of the dinner went just as delightful. We talked about our individual, growing businesses and future babies… again. Khalil and I cut the cake while the photographer snapped our pictures.

After cutting the cake, my father, Aidan, Khalil's father, Kadesh, and Khalil went out by the pool to smoke celebratory cigars while the women talked, and ZaNita's company cleaned up our completed meal and stored away the top of our cake.

Early in the week, we invited some friends and colleagues to come over this evening for an impromptu reception. We didn't tell them at first what it was, so when they made it over this evening, everybody was shocked and upset we married without them present. Nevertheless, it was a magical night to remember.

Khalil and I danced our first dance as husband and wife to Major "Why I Love You". My husband sang in my ear while the whole room watched us embrace in a slow dance. I was so in love with him it should be illegal. We drank with family and friends until the wee hours of the morning, then crashed when the sun came up the next morning. It was the best wedding ever.

✳✳✳

"Yes, place those over on the table next to the buffet. They're going to be for the candy-bar centerpiece," I said to my assistant.

I have been here in Las Vegas for three days now. The event that I was planning was a ballroom sweet-sixteen party theme "Golden Princess" for the daughter of a best-selling author I met at a book signing. My networking skills were top notch.

DoubleD: *Hello, my hard-working wife… I miss you. *kissy face emoji**

Instantly, the little stress I was feeling started to evaporate. This was the first time Khalil and I had been apart since we got married last month. He'd been working locally, and so have I for the most part, but money talks, and duty called. The mother of the young lady, whose birthday it was, paid an extra twenty thousand dollars to get me to come do this party, so I made sure to show up and not send my staff only.

Me: *I miss you so much, baby! I'll be home before you know it.*

DoubleD: *Not soon enough. *sad face emoji**

Me: *How was your day?*

DoubleD: *It was busy as ever. I just got in this lonely ass bed all alone… When is my wife bringing her sexy ass home?*

Me: *I'll be home tomorrow. You know that my flight lands at six in the evening.*

DoubleD: *So another whole day, Ajah… Naw. I'll send the jet to come get you in* *the morning.*

With that, I called him.

Ring! Ring!

"There is no use in you trying to talk me out of it. I'm sending the plane at eight in the morning, and you better be on it when it comes back to the private strip here in Texas, where I'll be waiting at ten thirty," Khalil said before I could get a word out.

"Baby, I can't. I have final venue completion and closure tomorrow. Why are you being unreasonable like we've never traveled for work before? What's going on?" I asked, a little annoyed.

"We weren't together and married then, Ajah. I'm horny and in need of my wife. All that other shit you talking is irrelevant. Why can't your assistant do completion tomorrow?"

"Ugh… Khalil, really? You don't think if I could, I would. I'm missing you too, but baby, you need to be patient for me. Pleaseeee," I whined.

"Listen. I don't want to hear all that. You've been gone for three days already, and you want me to wait to see you until tomorrow evening. Naw. That's a big no for me. You need to figure it out and be home before noon tomorrow, or the jet won't be coming alone. I will be on it too."

"Baby… Bookie… this is my livelihood. You knew what I did before we got married. Why you tripping now? What's really going on?"

"Ajah, I love you. Do what I say, okay? Stop trying to debate. You know what's up."

He was right. I did know because I was feeling the same desires and lonesomeness without him in bed holding me. I could get my assistant to do completion tomorrow. However, I had some other business ventures that I was looking into, and the meeting was set for one o'clock tomorrow afternoon. It would be unprofessional to cancel now at seven o'clock in the evening the night before.

"Khalil, please just cut me some slack. I miss you more than you know, but I have other business to tend to," I slightly begged on edge, thinking about how he was going to respond.

After a couple minutes of just listening to each other breathe, he said, "Look, I know you're at the venue since the party is tonight. Just video call me when you get back to your room, okay?"

"Okay, baby," I said in a sobering tone. "I love you husband."

"I love you more, wife. Talk to you soon."

"Soon," was all I replied, and then I hung up.

I wanted to cry. He had no idea how much I was missing him too. I knew when he started traveling for work again, I'd be a lot worse than he just was… big facts. However, I knew what our business lives were like, so we both had to bite the bullet.

After hanging up with Khalil, I threw myself into finishing up the decorations at the venue, making sure the caterers were in place and the food was being prepared correctly, organizing last-minute music changes with the DJ, calling the client, making sure her daughter was satisfied with her grand entrance accommodations, and getting the guest list to the bouncers at the doors.

By the time I comfortable leaving the venue to my staff, it was eleven o'clock at night, and I was tired. On the way to the Bellagio, where I was staying, I texted Khalil to let him know I was on my way to the hotel to shower and that I would be video calling him. He didn't respond. I knew it was because he was upset, but I'd make it up to him by calling him naked when I got to the room.

As I was sitting in the back of the town car, scrolling through my emails, I came across an article from Shavonne with the subject line, *girl, you see this shit!*

Club Iconic owner, Malachi Richardson, was found dead inside of the office of his latest nightclub here in West Palm Beach. Janet Cummings, his assistant manager, found him when she came into the club to start opening up for tonight's scheduled grand-opening event. No word yet on cause of death. His manager stated that the cameras were set to be functioning beginning tonight, so no surveillance is available just yet. We will keep updating as we get information.

Oh my goodness! That's so sad! I called Shavonne. "Girlllll... What the heck y'all have going on in Florida?"

"Babeee! When I saw that article, I was like thank goodness you got away from him when you did. Ain't no telling what he was caught up in opening up a new night club every month. People aren't clubbing that hard... child boo," Shavonne said all animated. I could imagine what she looked like as she was talking, hands and arms moving faster than her mouth.

"Girl, who you telling? I definitely dodged a bullet with that stalker. If he kept going the way he was at me, fucking with Khalil, that would've been his fate sooner anyway," I said, joking but knew good and well my man didn't play. He was quiet but deadly.

"Ohh! Passion, I forgot all about that. You don't think... You know rumor is his neck was broken. What if—"

"No, I don't think, and you don't either," I said, cutting her off before she says something stupid.

"Mmmhmm!" she said all sarcastically.

"Anyway, trick, whatchu up to?" I asked, happily changing the subject.

"Just leaving this business dinner with my lawyer for a company here. They want me to design a fashion app for this Instagram model. We were talking those digits." She bragged.

My bestie was the best tech and gaming engineer in the south. Her vivid vision of life's adventures and color made her successful at designing and building apps, as well as games, for many big-name companies.

"Look at you bossing. Don't forget the little people when you get to the top," I said.

Sucking her teeth, she said, "This coming from the woman planning celebrity bachelor parties for NBA stars and married to a billionaire… stop fronting." She sassed.

"Whatever!" I joked. "Well, I've made it to my hotel. I'll call you tomorrow. I gotta go shower and call my man before he flies to Vegas to drag me home by my curls."

"That's my big bro. Ain't nobody tell you to be grown and leave him for three days, knowing your ass having withdrawals too."

"Gurrrrllllll… mmmm… You have no idea!"

"And I don't want one either. Talk to you later. Love you, sis," she said with a laugh.

"Love you mo… later," I said, blowing her a smooch through the phone.

Walking into the hotel with my face in my phone and my mind so focused on what I just read and heard from Shavonne, along with my thoughts of the possibility that Khalil had something to do with Malachi's death, I bumped hard into a stranger on my way to the elevator.

"So sorry, excuse me," I said as I felt a strong arm catch me. I looked up. "Khalil…" I whispered.

With his arm still wrapped around me, he took his other one to cuff my butt and lift me up. I wrapped my legs around him, and we walked through the hotel. Once we reached the elevators, both his hands were gripping my ass with my legs and arms wrapped around his waist and neck. He kissed me softly on the lips.

"Fuck, I missed you, woman," he groaned, laying his forehead on mine.

"I missed you too," I manage to get out through a moan right before my back was pressed against the elevator wall, and his lips were covering mine. My hips began moving on their own accord, creating a friction between our bodies that had my pussy jumping out my pants. "Kh… Khalil, baby… wait," I mumbled as his lips were now sucking my own.

Halting, Khalil asked, "Wait for what, Ajah?"

"What are you doing here? Why didn't you tell me you were coming here?" The tightness of his hands slackened. I tightened my legs around his waist. "Khalil, don't, please. I'm just surprised. You know I'm happy you're here. I would've been here sooner if I knew you were waiting," I said with an obvious plea.

Silence. Then deep exhales.

"I know you didn't mean anything by it. I'm not upset. My mind just all over the place, there's a lot going on at work recently, and I need my serenity… my peace… you! But check that tone, because you were about five seconds from getting a spanking in this damn elevator," he said with a smirk.

"Whatever you freak." I laughed.

Ding!

Finally, the elevator reached my floor. We walked off with me still in my husband's arms and my face buried in his neck.

"Mmmm," I murmured as I take in his scent through my nostrils.

When we make it to my room's door, without me telling him where it is might I add—to which I'm not surprised—Khalil slid his own keycard into the slot to open the door. I just chuckled and shook my head.

Inside the room, near the door, sat Khalil's overnight bag. Khalil pats me on the butt, signaling for me to get down. I slid down the front of his body making sure to rub myself vigorously against him. Once I am on my feet, he grabbed the side of my face and placed the most impassioned kiss slowly on my lips. We both smiled as we pulled away.

"I'll start the shower. You hungry or want to head to bed after?" he asked over his shoulder on the way to the bathroom.

"No, thank you. I ate already. Unless you're hungry... I'm good. I just want to get clean and lay up under my man," I yell out as I walked over to the side of the bed and stood near the nightstand to take off my jewelry.

I could hear the shower behind me being turned on. I took a deep breath. I was exhausted. It was a long day. As I began to lift my blouse over my head, my hands are moved out of the way, and Khalil replaced them with his own and began to undress me. I can feel his body heat on my bare back, which could only mean he's already undressed, I start to turn my head 'cause I can't get enough of the view of him naked.

"Face forward," he commanded.

With my bottom lip between my teeth, I say with a smile, "Yes, sir."

Next, to go down was my zipper, and then he pulled down my skirt along with my panties. Crouched down behind me, he places a kiss on both my ass cheeks. I gasped and closed my eyes. With his hand is on my lower back, I felt the pressure of him bending my body forward, making my chest touch the bed. He licked me from my pussy to my ass, going up and down, making my knees buck.

"Oh, God!" I yell out.

Moving lower, he penetrated my folds, back and forth, touching my clit with just the tip of his tongue. He went from the front to back repeatedly, teasing me, getting me closer and closer to climax. I began matching his pace. Standing on my tippy-toes, I bounced my ass up and down... back and forth.

Khalil never slowed down his rhythm. He continued to lick me. I felt my juices leaking down my thighs. He began fucking my pussy with his masterful tongue. His thumb moves to my asshole, and then he penetrated it. I jumped slightly. His hand put more pressure on my lower back.

"I'm cumming. Don't stop."

He moved his thumb out of my rear, reached around my waist, and used his forefinger and thumb to pinch my clit. I explode, squirting my juices all over his face. Weakened, I collapsed on the bed… feet flat. Khalil licked my juices up from my body like it was his daily smoothie, then kissed my ass cheeks one at a time.

Smacking me on the butt as he comes up from his crouching position, I turned my head to the side to look at him. He was naked like I assumed. I reached back and grab his cock in my hand and began to massage it up and down. He's so hard. He moved my hand from around him, spread my legs wider with his knee, and slid into home. We both groaned as he slowly filled me. He starts slow stroking.

"You good?" he asked.

"Yes… harder, baby… harder," I begged.

Widening his legs, he did just that—went harder with both his hands now gripping my waist. I gained my footing and proceeded to throw that ass back. In and out, powerful thrusts came from my husband. He's in full beast mode, and I'm in ecstasy. I pushed back into him. I needed him so deep I could taste him in my mouth.

"Fuck, Ajah," he grunted out.

I felt him pulsating in me. "You feel so good, daddy. I'm close… Cum with me."

Making an animalistic sound, he went harder… deeper. "I'm there, baby… Cum with me, baby," Khalil said in a grunt.

Mid-orgasm I push back on him with all the strength I have left. He stumbled and fell out of me. I dropped down to my knees, put him in my mouth, and started sucking the magnificent, mushroom head of his cock.

"Ajjahhhh," he moaned.

His hand went in my hair while he pumped his hips for a few more seconds, and then he released in my mouth. His cum was sweet and thick. Moaning, I swallowed it all, not missing a drop. I opened my eyes and looked up at him.

Licking my lips, I said, "Tastes just like candy."

He rubbed his fingers through my hair and smiled. "I fucking love you, woman."

"I love you more, my king," I said, still licking my lips.

Showering with Khalil was one of my greatest pleasures. The way we'd steal touches while pampering each other was intimacy at its best. That night, we both crashed as soon as our bodies connected with the bed. Khalil slept with his head underneath my breasts and his arms tightly encased around my waist.

I was worried about him. Although his demeanor was normal, his eyes showed stress that I wasn't used to seeing in his eyes. Could Shavonne be on to something? Did my husband have a hand in Malachi's death?

I know Malachi was becoming a nuisance, but I didn't think the situation was that serious. Of course, I'd never accuse Khalil of anything like that, but

I knew him, and pride plus ego could be deathly if provoked.

I just wanted my man back to himself, and I had to find a way to get him there.

CHAPTER 21

Inhale.
Exhale.
Inhale.
Deep exhale.
Panting.

Sweat dripping down my back and chest. Soreness in my legs. Tightness in my thighs. Walking into the house from my run, I was feeling more exhausted than I ever had before. I was in shape, ran eight miles four days a week. I couldn't understand why my body was reacting this way. Nausea rose again. I'd already thrown up on the park trail, which was super embarrassing. Now here I was again on the verge of throwing up. I raced to the bathroom downstairs, barely making it before this yellow, thick substance came out of my mouth. *Ewww.*

For the next fifteen minutes, my head was making friends with the porcelain god. After I made sure everything was done, I got up to wash my mouth and face.

"This is not happening," I said to myself out loud. Khalil was at work. Thank goodness, but I knew what I had to do.

✳✳✳

"Mrs. Black how are you doing today?" asked my primary physician, Dr. Swanson.

"Not good. I've been throwing up for the past week and feeling very fatigued," I replied.

"Any other symptoms? Cough, headache, congestion, anything of that sort?" she asked while checking my ears, nose, throat, and vitals.

"No, ma'am," I replied.

"Mrs. Black—"

I cut her off. Her calling me Mrs. Black felt weird 'cause she was clearly older than me. I appreciated the respect, but it still felt weird. "You can call me, Ajah," I said.

"Sure," she replied with bewilderment all over her facial expression. "Ajah, when was the last day of your last menstrual cycle?"

"Two Thursdays ago, on the nineteenth." I knew that was going to be her first thought. It was mine as well, but I hadn't missed a cycle.

"Alright, I'm going to send the nurse back in. We're going to take some blood and urine to run some tests. Any pain or discomfort anywhere?" she asked while placing her hand on my stomach and applying a little pressure.

"I've had some in my lower abdomen a couple days ago, like a light cramping, but I chalked it up to gas. It passed after a few minutes and hasn't come back." I shrugged.

"Okay, take a deep breath for me... and release. Good. Again. Good. You're not wheezing, and I don't hear any congestion. Let me get the nurse in here, and we'll start the testing process, okay, Ajah?" she said with the warmest smile.

"Yes, ma'am. Thank you," I replied.

After providing the nurse with my blood and urine, I sat in the exam room and waited. Since I was antsy, I decided to distract myself with work.

Ping!

My phone alerted me of a text. It was Khalil.

"Fuck! He's gonna want to know where I am," I mumbled to myself.

Hubby: *Hey, baby. How is your day going?*

Me: *I'm good. Just out at Michaels, shopping for a centerpiece for this event next week.*

Hubby: *Word? Which one? I have a long break before my next patient. Let's go to lunch.*

Shit! I didn't want him to worry, so I didn't tell him I was sick. *Think, Ajah. Think.*

Me: *Babe, I'm all the way in Azle. They had a sale at this one. I'll just see you tonight at home.*

Hubby: *Ajah, don't play with me. What's going on?*

Me: *Why something has to be going on?*

Hubby: *Because I know you're not in Azle. Don't make me hurt you. Where are you?*

Ugh! He made me sick. How he know I'm not in Azle? When I didn't immediately reply, my phone started ringing.

"Yes, stalker?" I answered.

"Where are you? If you lie to me again, there'll be consequences," Khalil stated.

Exhaling loudly, I murmured, "I'm at Dr. Swanson's office."

"What! See I knew something was wrong. I'll be there in ten minutes," he said, being all dramatic.

"No, Khalil. I'm fine, just feeling under the weather. Don't make a big deal," I pleaded.

"I'll be there in a few minutes." Without a goodbye he hung up. He was mad, mad.

Twelve minutes later, Khalil walked into the exam room with that sexy, cocky stride I loved so much.

"Hey, baby," I said, trying to get brownie points.

"What's up?" he replied with a frown. He walked over to me and grabbed my face between his hands, then kissed me on the lips. With his forehead resting on mine and his eyes closed, he asked, "The doctor come back in yet?"

"How you know I saw the doctor already?" I said with a smirk, shaking my head.

"If you haven't, there's about to be a problem." As soon as he said that, there was a knock on the door.

"Come in," I answered. Khalil moved to my left, beside the bed.

"Oh! We have a guest. Hello. I'm Dr. Swanson," she said, reaching out to shake Khalil's hand.

"Khalil Black," he replied all dry and shook her outstretched hand.

"Ajah, we have your test results back in. I apologize for the delay," Dr. Swanson said with a huge smile on her face. *I'm sick. What the hell she smiling at?* I thought to myself "We were able to find the source of your recent fatigue, nausea, and pain."

"What pain? Why have you been keeping this from me, baby? I'm a doctor. You don't trust your husband's opinion?" Khalil said clearly upset.

"Really, Khalil? Right now you wanna do this? I'm sorry, Dr. Swanson. Please continue," I said, giving him that "chill" look. She had that smile on her face again. *WTF?*

"Absolutely. As I was saying, all your tests came back, and we were able to conclude that the reason you're having all these symptoms is because you're pregnant!" Her smile was even bigger now.

"Pregnant!" Khalil and I said in unison.

"But I've still been having my cycle?" I asked, not understanding how this was possible.

"Which is not uncommon. Describe your recent cycle to me," Dr. Swanson stated.

"Light, about two to three days for the past couple months." I was so confused at this point.

When I said that, Khalil threw his arms around me, squeezing me super tight, and then he placed a deep, impassioned kiss on my lips. His tongue broke through, and his hands went to the back of my neck as he deepened the kiss. I moaned and grabbed the lapel of his suit jacket—I needed something to anchor me before I floated away.

"I love you... I love you... I love you... Thank you, baby," Khalil said between placing kisses on my lips. "We're pregnant." I felt wetness on my cheek. Pulling back, I looked at Khalil, and he was crying.

"Baby," I whispered.

"I love you, Ajah. You and my seed are my world. I love you. Thank you, baby. I'm going to be a daddy!" he shouted like we weren't at the doctor's office. I laughed. His hand went to my stomach as he pecked me on the lips again.

"I love you too, daddy," I said full of joy.

Finally remembering where we were I looked around Khalil for Dr. Swanson, but we were alone. She must've realized we needed privacy.

According to my bloodwork, Dr. Swanson determined I was between twelve to sixteen weeks, which meant I got pregnant around the first time Khalil and I had sex—worthless ass birth control. To get an accurate time, I would have to see an ob-gyn. However, my gynecologist wasn't good enough for Khalil. He wanted to utilize someone he knew was top notch, so I allowed him to pick my ob-gyn, and we scheduled our first appointment. Of course, because of who I married, we were able to get in right away, which just made Khalil's week.

CHAPTER 22

"Hello, Mr. and Mrs. Black. I am Dr. Anderson." She was a beautiful, black woman that looked to be in her mid-forties. *Where did Khalil find her?* I wondered. "Congratulations on your new addition!" she said with a warming smile.

"Thank you," we both replied.

"How are you feeling, Mrs. Black?" Dr. Anderson asked.

"You can call me, Ajah," I said. *Here we go again.* "I'm feeling alright. Still some nausea and tiredness, especially when I work out, but other than that, nothing has really changed."

"I noticed that she's not eating as much, and when she sleeps, it's not peaceful. She's tossing and turning a lot," Khalil said, adding his two cents.

"I noticed Dr. Swanson put you on anti-nausea medicine. Are they not working?" Dr. Anderson asked.

"I'm not sure. I still vomit, but it's down to once a day, so I guess that's an improvement."

It had only been a week since we'd seen Dr. Swanson, so the decrease was amazing, but I was already over this morning sickness.

"Okay, are there any other concerns, from either one of you?" she asked, looking between Khalil and me.

"Not me," I answered.

"Will we be getting a due date today?" asked Khalil.

"Yes, we will, as well as doing a preliminary ultrasound, which we'll start with right now. Mrs. Bla—excuse me, Ajah, let's get you undressed from the waist down for the exam. I'll be returning shortly with the ultrasound tech." With that, she walked out the room.

"Khalil, why you being so mean to that lady? You picked her, so what's the problem?" I asked as he helped me get off the exam table so I could get undressed like Dr. Anderson instructed.

"I'm not being mean, baby. I'm just ready for us to speed this along so I can know what's going on with our baby. She keeps asking all these questions It's aggravating."

I laughed at him. "It's a part of the exam, baby. Chill out. You're worse than our mothers. Goodness."

We decided to go ahead and tell our parents about the pregnancy when we first found out, and of course they were already picking out baby names and looking for property to buy here in Texas, which scared the crap out of me because I knew they were serious. We'd all be neighbors soon. Shavonne was also ecstatic and kept saying, "I'm an auntie!" over and over again.

After about five minutes, Dr. Anderson walked back in with a petite, black woman, who introduced herself as Brittani. She was the ultrasound tech. Succeeding introductions, Brittani placed the gel on my "I'm full and just ate" looking stomach and began the ultrasound.

We were thirteen weeks and one day. My due date was May 4, 2020. Khalil squeezed my hand, kissed my face, and inappropriately gripped my hair as he stood next to the bed, and we listened to the beautiful sound of our baby's heartbeat. It was a moment I'd never forget. My heart opened up to its widest crest, and I fell in love with our blessing in that moment.

On the ride home, Khalil drove with his left hand on the steering wheel and his right hand remained on my stomach.

"What's on your mind, baby?" I asked, rubbing the hand he had on my stomach.

"You got pregnant the first time we made love," he said with a huge grin on his face.

I chuckled. "I was thinking that too. Like what the hell happened to my birth control? I've never missed a shot!"

"I told you how ineffective those things were when you started getting them. I'm glad you were too lazy to take the pill, but I told you that was the best choice."

Of course, he was glad my birth control didn't work. I was happy too, but a part of me was nervous. We'd just gotten married.

"You don't think it's too soon?" I asked Khalil.

"Too soon for what, Ajah? We've known each other practically our entire lives. I've been in love with you since I was old enough to know what love is. I think I waited too long. I should have been man'd up and made you mine, but now that I have you, I don't want nothing slowing us down. This baby is our blessing and just the beginning. I'm gonna make it my mission to keep you filled with my seeds."

"Why did you wait so long to ask me for more?" I'd been wanting to ask him that since we started dating.

"Seriously, I wanted us both to explore life first because I knew once I made you mine. I was going to be your last, just like I was your first." He glanced over at me and smirked. *Cocky ass.*

I sat there blushing because I knew what he said was true. That night at FAMU, when he gave me him and took me, was the night we took each other's virginity, and it was the best day of my life. No other lover had every compared, no matter how hard I tried to mask what I felt and forget it.

"For what it's worth, I'm glad you finally took the steps to make our *we* an *us*. I feel like the chance we took by giving us a chance at more is the best decision I made in my life. I love you so much, Khalil, and I'll give you however many babies you want," I said, leaning over the console to give him a kiss.

CHAPTER 23

December 2019

"Oh, God! Yes, baby! That feels so good! Don't stop," I moaned with my eyes rolling back in my head.

I was now twenty-two weeks—five months—and I was huge. It was like I woke up one morning, and my stomach got out of the bed before me. Khalil was overjoyed with my new belly. I was torn because now I couldn't fit any of my clothes. Good news about it all was, according to Dr. Anderson, we were only having one baby. I found out my mother's mother had a twin that died at birth, and my little angel was growing well. I had two more weeks before I knew what we were having, and I couldn't wait to find out.

"You like that, huh?" Khalil asked, smiling.

"You know I do," I replied. "So how was work today? When is your next event?"

"Hey, fella, multitask. Don't stop massaging these feet 'cause you talking." We laughed, and he resumed the glorious task known as a foot massage. "I have three events next week and one the week after, and then I have no events scheduled until February."

He exhaled loudly. "When are you going to slow down, baby? You're with child... our child. All this running around and stuff is going to have to slow down. What are your plans for when the baby gets here?"

"I haven't thought about it, Khalil. We still have four and a half more months to go," I replied, annoyed. He was continuously trying to get me to slow down like I was handicapped now that I was pregnant.

"How about I hire more staff for you so you can slow down?" he asked.

"Khalil, please don't start that. I'm pregnant not handicapped."

"I know you're not handicapped. I remember that ride this morning." He winked. *Nasty self.*

"Whatever, nasty. I promise to slow down or hire more staff the further down along in my pregnancy, okay?" I said as I blew him a kiss.

"For now, yes." He wasn't buying my attempt at manipulation.

"Thank you, sir," I said, flirting with him. I was horny again, and he was going to give me some dick.

"Ajah, you ready again, baby?" he said, licking his lips.

"Yessss," I said in my sexy voice.

"Come here," he demanded. I pulled my feet from his lap and crawled over to him on the couch and straddled his lap. "What you want, baby? Tell me." Khalil teased, grabbing me by my neck like I liked it.

"I want you deep inside your pussy," I said in a moan.

I leaned in and kissed him on the lips, sucking on his tongue and biting his bottom lip. He broke our kiss, then pulled my nightgown over my head. I was bare underneath.

Moving back a little, I went for the waistband of his pants. He lifted up to help me get them down enough to spring his erection free. I licked my lips. His dick was so fucking gorgeous. I moved back up his body so that I was right on top of him and starting to inch myself down. I knew I was already wet. That was another perk of pregnancy. I was always soaked and ready.

"Ohhhh... mmmm," I moaned.

Khalil's hands were on my waist, and he was slowly thrusting up. "Fuck, baby. You're so wet. Damn, Ajah."

My head fell to his shoulder. I was now completely sheathing his love muscle. We began to move, establishing that perfect rhythm that only we had together. Up and down. Up and down. Khalil guided me with his hands on my waist and gifted me with his thrusts from below. I threw my head back and bounced harder.

"That's right, baby. Take this dick!"

I loved when he talked dirty to me during sex—such a turn on. We were panting and thrusting and bouncing out of control. I could feel my muscles tightening around him while he pulsed within me.

"Khalilll…" I was begging for release.

He sat up and placed my breast in his mouth and sucked my nipple. I moved my hand from his shoulder and pulled him more into my chest. He moaned and sucked harder. Removing one of his hands from my waist, he smacked my ass hard, and I exploded losing my rhythm, and I started vibrating.

Khalil didn't miss a beat. He kept his pace thrusting inside of me until he found his release with my name on his lips "Ajah…" he growled.

We were in the same spot for about five minutes, with Khalil still inside of me, kissing my neck and rubbing my back. All of a sudden, he stood up, still holding me, and we walked up the stairs just like that, with me wrapped around my husband. I was too tired and ready for bed, so Khalil washed my body while we stood in the shower, quickly washed himself, and then we retired to our bed. I slept as I had been the past two months since we found out we were pregnant, with his face in my neck and his hand on my stomach. Pure bliss.

CHAPTER 24

January 2020

Today was the day we found out what we were having. I was now twenty-seven weeks and looked like I was nine months. We had to wait an additional three weeks from the expected date because Khalil had a patient that got injured while vacationing in the Dominican Republic, so Khalil and I went to the DR. Yes, I had to go too. My husband refused to go without me.

While he treated his patient, I enjoyed the beaches in my bikini. We utilized the island and took a week vacation, causing us to reschedule our ultrasound. However, today was the day, and to say I was anxious was an understatement. I couldn't wait to see my fatty cakes. For me to be this big I'm sure we'd get some awesome pictures. I hadn't had an ultrasound since I was thirteen weeks, and I was ready to see my baby.

"Baby, you want to stop and get anything to eat before we get to the doctor?" Khalil asked as he drove to the doctor's office. He recently purchased a 2020 Audi Q7 for me so that I would have an easier ride to get into, and I was loving this car, just hated driving right now.

"Nah, I'm good, baby. I ate a sandwich before we left the house," I replied.

"A sandwich?" he asked skeptically.

"Don't do me please. This is your greedy, giant baby, so if I ate three turkey-and-cheese grilled sandwiches, it's all your fault," I said, laughing.

"I'm witchu when you're right, baby," he responded, reaching over and rubbing my stomach. I pulled his hand from my stomach and kissed the inside of his palm then stuck his forefinger in my mouth and begin sucking on it. "Ajah… baby, what you got going on? Don't make me turn this truck around. I want to see my daughter," he said with a smirk.

"I think you're gonna be shamed because this is your son, darling," I said over his finger, then commenced to sucking it harder.

"We'll see," he said, taking his finger out of my mouth and moving it to my breast, then tugging on my nipple ring.

"Sssssss… KJ, mmmmm." I laid my head back on the seat, closed my eyes, and released my body to him. He pulled and twisted my nipple at a steady tempo, round and round… in and out. My pelvis was pumping the air back and forward. "Ahhhh… fuckkkk… Khalil!"

Rockets launched, my body shook, and I exploded. No vaginal penetration, no licking to my pussy, just my husband's skillful fingers on my sensitive nipples. Fuck, he's a magician.

Opening my eyes, I turn my head to look at my baby. He had this triumphant smile on his handsome face.

"You good?" he asked.

"Hmmmm." I nodded, still unable to speak.

He leaned over the center console and planted a deep, wet, juicy kiss on my lips, then pulled back and looked me in the eyes. "Good," was his reply.

He starts getting out of the truck, and it was then I realize that we were at the doctor's office. He walked around to my side, opened my door, and took my hand, helping me out of the car. I wobbled on my legs for a brief moment. Khalil tilted his head and frowned down at me.

"You're the one that made me cum," I said matter-of-factly.

He chuckled and kissed me on the lips, then bent down and kissed my belly while he said, "Your mama is a freak." We both laugh.

"Don't tell my baby that, clown," I said, laughing still.

"Come on before we're late," he said, intertwining our hands.

With big smiles on our faces, we walked into the doctor's office to see our precious baby.

***

"Twins? A-Are you sure?" I asked Dr. Anderson. Khalil still hadn't said a word.

"Yes, I'm sure. If you look at the screen, you'll see that they are in the same sac. That is probably how we missed one at your thirteen-week ultrasound. However, they both look very healthy. All their limbs are developing very well. Here are the spines, fingers, and toes, and they have strong heartbeats. According to the ultrasound, baby A weighs 3lb, and baby B here is 2lbs. Would you like to know the sexes?" she asked.

I turned to my left to see how Khalil was taking this news. He still had not said a word. "Babe, you okay?"

"Huh?" he replied, still staring at the screen.

"Dr. Anderson asked if we want to know the sexes of the babies." He just nodded his head up and down.

"I know it's a shock, but the good news is they are both healthy and growing on schedule according to your due date," Dr. Anderson said encouragingly.

"Khalil?" He looked at me and smiled. "Yes, Dr. Anderson, we'd like to know the sexes," I answered for us both.

"Alright let's see what we have here. Okay, if you would both look at the screen in front of you again, you'll see the legs, and rightttt there between the legs is... It's boys!!!" she said with a huge smile on her face.

"Yes!" I shouted and raised my arms above my head.

The babies started moving around a lot like they were trying to switch places, and you could see it on the screen clear as day.

"I have sons... I have sons, Ajah," Khalil said, staring at the screen.

"Yes, baby, you have two sons." I chuckled at him being speechless.

He looked over at me, stepped closer to the bed, and pulled me into a deep, toe-curling kiss. By the time we came up for air, the doctor was out of the room. *She's gonna kick us out next time I bet.* I was panting trying to catch my breath.

"Thank you, baby," Khalil whispered in my ear.

"Don't thank me. You put them in there." At that we both burst out laughing.

"Come on. Let's go make your next appointment so we can go home, and I can show you just how grateful I am," Khalil said as he licked my ear.

I never got dressed so fast in my life! I grabbed the ultrasound pictures the doctor must've left when we were preoccupied with each other's mouths, and we headed for the door.

Standing at the counter making my next appointment, I heard behind me, "Well, look who we have here."

Khalil and I turned around and came face-to-face with a constant headache. *Here the fuck comes the drama,* I thought to myself.

"Hello, Destiny," I said, not giving Khalil the chance to even entertain her thot ass.

Just as I said that, a handsome, dark-skinned man covered in tattoos came up behind her and wrapped his arm around her waist and placed his hands on her stomach. I was so caught up in her presence that I did not notice her small baby belly. I looked over at Khalil, but he was looking at the guy behind her like he knew him.

"A girl! I got me a princess coming!" the tattoo-covered hottie stated, obviously overjoyed and kissed her on the neck. Then he looked up at us and said, "Hello. How y'all doing?"

"We're doing wonderful. Thank you for asking. Congratulations on your baby girl!" Khalil said, standing protectively in front of me now like he thought the guy was going to snatch or kidnap me. *What was going on here?*

"Thanks, man. What y'all having, if you don't mind me asking?" he asked Khalil in a friendly tone.

"Twin boys!" Khalil responded with the biggest smile on his face that I'd ever seen.

Destiny's mouth was hanging wide open, and her eyes was watery like she wanted to cry. Clearing her throat, she said, "Come on, Choppa. Let's go, baby. I'm hungry."

"Sure, baby. Nice meeting y'all, and congratulations on the boys. That's what's up," he said with a head nod.

"Thank you," Khalil and I said in unison. I looked at Khalil.

"That was almost you," I said with a sarcastic smirk on my face.

Frowning, he said, "The hell it was. I know how to double up. I always knew there was only one woman that was going to carry my seeds, and now she's giving me two." He winked at me and kissed my cheek.

"Damn, you smooth," I said, shaking my head.

"Naw, I'm smart. Now come on. My tongue itching for some Ajah."

"Nasty self," I said as I chuckled.

"Only for you, baby… Only for you," he said, grabbing me over my shoulder and kissing me on the neck right below my ear, then sucking on my earlobe.

"Sssssss… Khalil, baby," I moaned.

"Yeah, bring yo' ass." He smacked my ass and walked off.

Khalil made me drive home, which took us forty-five minutes on a twenty-minute drive because he wanted to eat pussy as an appetizer before we got home for him to eat his entrée—his words, not mine. It was the best forty-minute slow drive home ever.

CHAPTER 25

Before we could make it out of the car into the house, I was calling my mother.

"Hello, Passion. How did the appointment go?" was how my mother answered the phone. No hello for her daughter. Always about the pregnancy now.

"Ma, they say I'm having twins… twins!" I said, still kinda in shock.

"What! How could that be? I thought there has only been one heartbeat at appointments and only one on the first ultrasound?" I could hear the fake panic in her voice.

"Apparently, they are so in sync that it seems like one. I don't know, Ma, but Dr. Anderson said one was hiding behind his brother."

"Ohhhhhh my goodness! They're boys!" I heard her clapping her hands and shouting for my daddy at the same time.

"I don't believe this," I mumbled.

Khalil grabbed my hand. "What, baby?"

"She's celebrating with my daddy." He just laughs. Shaking my head, I returned my attention to the phone. "Mommy, I'll call you back." Before I can take the phone from my ear to disconnect, I heard my dad.

"Ajah! Baby, we're having twin boys! Oh, what a blessing!"

"That's what I keep hearing, Daddy." I pouted, now in full daddy's-girl mode—total brat.

"It is, baby girl. Your mother and I are booking a flight. We'll be there tomorrow." I got excited and nervous.

"Daddy, I could just ask Khalil if his plane is available. You guys don't have to spend the unnecessary money." I looked over at Khalil and asked, "My parents want to come visit. Can you send the plane tomorrow?"

Khalil response was immediate. "Absolutely. Anything you want, my love. Let me call my parents and see if they wanna make the trip as well." With that, he picked up his phone and called his parents. I knew exactly when he shared the news with them because I could hear his mother's scream from his side of the car. I laughed.

"Daddy, Khalil will call you with the flight details. Let me call Shavonne, and we'll make a celebration of it."

"Okay, baby girl. We love you. Tell Khalil your old man says, 'thank you'," he said, getting emotional.

"I will, Daddy. I love you." I was almost in tears myself.

"We love you more, angel." We hung up.

I looked over, and Khalil was staring at me intently. No words were necessary. I knew what he was feeling. The connection we shared was just that strong. He leaned over to kiss my tears away. I pulled back slightly, grabbed his face, and kissed him like my life depended on it. His tongue breaks through my lips, and I sucked on it as he grabbed me by the back of my neck and deepened the kiss.

Pulling back, he placed his forehead on mine. "We got this, baby," he said.

"I have no worries. Why would I? You're with me," I replied.

He kissed me on the forehead and turned to get out of the car. He came around to open my door and helped me out of the truck.

"Hungry?" Khalil asked.

"No, but I'm sleepy and horny."

He laughed. "What's new? I'm definitely enjoying this pregnancy. If they're all going to be like this, I'ma have to keep you loaded." I just burst out laughing.

"Nasty self."

"Only for you, baby… Only for you."

We spent the next few hours breaking in more walls in the house. I still couldn't believe that Khalil could hold me up while he drilled into me while I'm this big. I'd be in ecstasy and fear the entire time. My husband's strength was truly unmatched, and his energy was remarkable. I always ended up tapping out before him.

✳✳✳

It took two days for everyone to make it to Texas. My parents, Khalil's parents, and Shavonne came down all to celebrate the great news of our twins with us. Any reason to come visit and party was really the purpose if you ask me. Since they were already here I planned a small, early baby shower. Many of Khalil's and my colleagues, as well as friends we've made here in Texas, came out to bask in our joy.

"Girl, you surely know how to throw a party," said Shavonne as we sat by the pool, watching everybody mingle in the backyard.

"That is kind of what I do for a living, Sha," I said, chuckling at her comment.

"So how are you really taking the news?" she asked.

Shavonne knew me almost as well as Khalil. She was also my best friend. Those things I couldn't share with Khalil, I always took to Shavonne. I was beyond blessed.

"I'm scared and happy. With my business taking off like it is and Khalil traveling all the time, how are we going to juggle one, let alone two?"

Shavonne just looked at me for a few seconds, and then with a raised brow, she said, "You know damn well you got this. Plus, both y'all parents will be living down the street, and I'm only a flight away. You good."

"I know. I guess I'm just tripping." I pouted.

"No. You're pregnant, and it's okay. But we gotchu, mama, and Khalil will cease all travels for his family. You know that."

"Yeah, I know. I'm real lucky," I replied.

"Hey, did you ever ask him about the Malachi thing?" Shavonne asked.

I turned my head to look at her. "Heck no! I really don't want to know. Khalil is capable of many things, but I don't want to envision my husband in that capacity... even though I know it's possible. I don't want to know."

"Yeah, I feel ya! My bro is badass, but damn..." Shavonne said, shaking her head.

We left it at that. Khalil has a heart of gold. He's calm and very laid back, but he is also deadly when provoked, and Malachi poked him way too many times. Although a part of me felt like Khalil did handle Malachi, I didn't want to know, and I was sure he wouldn't tell me anyway. Therefore, it didn't matter because either way. I loved him, and I will continue to love him until my last breath.

EPILOGUE

One year later...

My boys were stubborn just like their father and beautiful like him too. I was the first woman with twins, that I knew of, that carried her babies almost full term. I went thirty-eight weeks before my angels decided to bless the world with their presence. I was on bed rest for the last three weeks of my pregnancy because my body could no longer sustain the weight, and my sciatic nerve was pinched, but they refused to come out, and my doctor saw no cause for induction, so I G'd up.

Of course, Khalil cancelled all future appointments and hired another doctor to monitor his patients so that he could wait on me hand and foot. Talk about the gift of a good man. My man was the epitome of what marriage is—commitment and unconditional love. I was blessed beyond my greatest imagination.

After being in labor for twenty-seven hours, my baby boys went into distress, and we had to do an emergency cesarean section. I was terrified for my babies and my husband, who presented a stupendous amount of strength and courage, but his eyes held water that never fell from his eyes.

Aiden Khalil Black was born six pounds, two ounces. My firstborn. A firecracker, he came out kicking and screaming. His twin, Kairo Evan Black, was born five pounds, seven ounces. My baby came out quiet and inquisitive. His eyes were wide open when the nurse let us look at him, but he never cried, just whimpered a little.

Who would've thought that the man I called my best friend would indeed be the love of my life? Khalil has inspired me to be something I would have never imagined—a loving wife and mother. I always thought I would end up an old maid, secretly in love with her best friend. Little did I know, we were in love with each other. I wouldn't change a thing about our journey together. I had a husband that was my best friend. Taking our relationship to the next level did not decrease our communication and trust in each other as friends. It nourished into a marriage beyond my most wildest dreams.

My kids made me a better person, and for them, I wanted to be more than I had ever been. My business was thriving, my marriage was blooming every day, and I was the happiest woman in the universe, thanks to the three most important guys in my life—Khalil, Aiden, and Kairo.

DENOUEMENT

Khalil - Five years later...

Standing outside of our closet, watching my sexy wife get dressed for our date night, was more pleasurable than the show we were scheduled to watch. After six years of companionship and a lifetime in friendship together, she was still the most beautiful woman in the world to me. A magnificent mother to our five-year-old twins, Kairo and Aiden, she made life worth living for all of us every day.

Both our businesses were thriving these days. Although Ajah had pulled back from the field and most of her planning is from our home office, she was still very proactive in Exquisite Events' daily operations. Having her work from home was ideal. I'm not mad at that one at all. We needed her here, at home—in our home—because without her, this house malfunctioned. I'd slowed down my traveling as well, and on those rare occasions that I do travel, it always goes from work to a family vacation.

"You're going to make us late, Khalil, just standing there, baby. Finish getting dressed," Ajah stated.

She knew damn well I wasn't concerned with being late when I had her in my sights. I stepped all the way in the closet with my hands still in my pockets, like that was going to halt me from putting them everywhere on Ajah I could. I only had my slacks on, no shirt or shoes. When I saw my wife in the closet half-dressed standing at the closet island, my entire focus shifted to her body. Fuck putting on clothes. I was ready to take more off.

Ajah had on a black, lace bra and panties set I ordered her from Frederick's of Hollywood last month 'cause I wanted to see her in something revealing and classy, and damn if she didn't excel past my vision. Her belly was protruding over the panties, and her breasts were overflowing the bra. She was five months pregnant with my princess, and that made her look more beautiful than ever.

As I reached her, she looked at me out of her peripheral. "Khalil…" she started to protest, but I stopped her pleas with my lips.

Pulling her face into mine, I placed a wet, juicy kiss on her lips. Her hands went to my bare chest, and she pulled on my nipple rings. I felt the jolt of pain in my groin. Pulling back from the kiss, I began licking and sucking on her neck while I let my hands roam her body.

Moving my lips down to her breast, I sucked on her nipples, moving from one to the other, giving them both my undivided attention. My hands made their way below her belly and into her panties, and she moaned my name this time. My baby was soaked. I knew she wanted this too—she's at her horniest when she was pregnant. Her pussy already had that Aquafina flow, but when she was preggo, it quadrupled. I loved drinking from her sweet nectar, especially when she was wet like that. I bent down on my knees in front of her and ripped her panties from her body.

"Khalil… Really? Those are new," she whined like I gave a fuck.

I didn't respond with words. I responded by separating her lips with my nose and diving headfirst into my pussy. I felt her legs buck, so I caught her with my hands on her ass and continued my assault on her love tunnel.

My wife had the sweetest pussy in the world. It always tasted like a juicy, perfectly-ripe mango. I could eat from her for hours and never get full. Sucking on her clit, I felt her slack some more. She was leaking so much I was covered in it from my chin to my nose. The thought made me moan.

I licked her hole, fucking her with my tongue. Her hips start moving faster. Her hands now gripped my head, pulling my face into her. I knew she was almost there, and as soon as I suck that hard, delicious ass clit of her, she'd be pouring her nectar down my throat. I had other plans though, so I pulled my face back from her.

"Khalil! What the fuck? I was close!"

Again, I didn't respond with words. I stood up, slowly making sure to keep my hands on her in case her legs felt wobbly. I took one hand from her and moved her jewelry box outta my way. Taking both hands under her arms, I lifted her on the dresser.

"Open up," I demanded.

She widened her legs as I pulled my hard cock from my slacks. I didn't have the time to tease her. I was already leaking at the tip. I wanted inside my wife now. I stepped in between her legs and thrust inside my wife's tight, wet pussy. It took everything not to bust as soon as I felt her warmth.

It's true what they say—pregnant pussy will change your life. t's warmer, wetter, and tighter—at least mine is. I started to move at a slow pace as I looked directly into her eyes, making love to her mind and body. Her hands went to my shoulders, and she started grinding with me. We both groaned. I picked up the rhythm going harder. I owed her a few orgasms since I stopped the first one, so I could keep her on edge.

"Mmmm… You feel so good, baby," Ajah moaned.

"Show me how good… Give me the first one. Now, Ajah. Stop holding it." I knew my wife's body, and I knew she was being stubborn, so I pulled down the lace on one of her breasts and bit her nipple, then sucked it hard, pulling on her nipple ring. Instantly, I felt her tightening around me and exploding while screaming profanities.

"Yeah, there it goes. Give me a couple more, baby," I growled in her ear as I pulled her ass closer to the edge of the dresser and went deeper.

"Ahhhhhh… Khalil, baby… don't stop… I'm cum-cumming!"

This time, as she came, I swallow her screams with a kiss. She loved when I did this. She said it made her cum harder. I grunted in her mouth when I felt her nails in my back. She pulled back from the kiss and threw her head back as her body continued to shake. I pulled out and buried my face back in my pussy and suck on her clit. She has got to give me one more before I could nut.

"Baby… I can't…"

I ain't hearing that. I knew what her body could do because I've trained it to my will. I licked her from her pussy to her ass and back up to her clit. Her body has naturally reclined back further down onto the dresser.

As I suck on her clit, I placed two fingers inside her. I felt her tightening around my fingers. I took my other hand and massaged her breast that surely was sensitive. Her back arched off the dresser, and she orgasmed again, placing her hands on top of mine on her breast, squeezing tight. I lifted my head up to watch the marvelous sight of my wife climaxing and continued my motions in her pussy with my fingers until I could feel the tremors from her walls slacken.

"Can I get one mo?" I asked as I moved my fingers and hand to place my cock back to her dripping-wet heat.

I slowly work myself back into my wife's pussy, which was now tighter 'cause it's swollen. Placing my hands beside her on the dresser, I grinded and twisted my hips, trying to get her to climax with me. She opened her eyes, and we made contact.

"I love you," she said as she began to match my rhythm, placing her legs on the edge of the dresser while pushing her body up on her elbows, never breaking eye contact.

I admired my wife's strength. She was amazing. After three orgasms, I knew she was tired and wanted to rest, but she wouldn't until we both had orgasmed. I thrust harder into her with a grunt. Her pussy felt so fucking extraordinary, and I made sure I told her.

She moaned my name. She loved when I talked shit to her during sex. I felt my balls tightening up. I'm close. "Cum with me, baby. I'm so fucking close," I told her, pulling her closer, fucking her deeper and harder. "Give it to me, Ajah. Right now!" I commanded.

She moved miraculously, pushing her body all the way up, and I leaned more into her to meet her where she was forced to stop because of my daughter, and we kissed as we exploded together. *Muthafuckin' heaven.*

Ajah squeezed my neck like she was trying to anchor herself, but I got her, and I'd never let her fall. I moved my arms from her back and place them under her so I could carry her to the bed, and she wrapped her legs around my waist.

Kissing me on the neck, she mumbled, "I love you so much, Khalil

Black."

"I love you more, Mrs. Black."

After laying her down, I took her bra completely off. On my way to the bathroom to get us a washcloth, I took my pants off too. When I made it back to the bed, she was sprawled out over most of the California king.

"Baby, you can't sleep. We have the concert and dinner, remember?" I said as I wiped her up gently. I was met with silence. "Ajah? Baby?"

She turned her back to me and started snoring. She was tired now, and I felt bad because I knew she'd be tired after four orgasms. I just couldn't stop myself, and I didn't regret none of the pleasures we just shared.

I placed the washcloth on the nightstand and texted my mother-in-law to check on the boys. Both of our parents decided to move to Texas after the twins were born. It was a gift and a curse.

After she threatened my life and told me to leave them alone, I crawled in bed behind my wife and pulled her into my body. I could never get close enough. I needed her body on mine like I needed air to breathe.

"You owe me," Ajah murmured, moving her ass closer on my dick. If she wasn't so tired I'd fuck her again, right in this position. I'd give her a couple hours of rest.

"You know I always pay my debt. I gotchu, ma," I replied and kissed her neck.

Within seconds, we were both fast asleep.

I loved my life.

THE END

Coming Soon...

Fighting For Her Heart!

Shavonne's Story

Made in the USA
Columbia, SC
21 June 2019